THE BODY IN THE SWAMP

When several bodies are washed up in the swamplands of east Texas, the local police suspect drug-runners, and the Feds are called in to investigate — but can discover little. Possum Choa lives off the fat of the land, but his way of life is now threatened by the criminals infesting the area. With the help of his old friend Lena McCarver, possessed of mysterious powers of her own, and Police Chief Washington Shipp, Choa and the residents of the swamplands join forces to stop the evildoers once and for all.

ARDATH MAYHAR

THE BODY IN THE SWAMP

Complete and Unabridged

LINFORD
Leicester

First published in Great Britain

First Linford Edition
published 2016

A catalogue record for this book is available
from the British Library.

ISBN 978–1–4448–2916–7

Published by
F. A. Thorpe (Publishing)
Anstey, Leicestershire

Set by Words & Graphics Ltd.
Anstey, Leicestershire
Printed and bound in Great Britain by
T. J. International Ltd., Padstow, Cornwall

This book is printed on acid-free paper

1

Washington Shipp

Washington Shipp was hosing off the driveway when Jewel, his wife, called him to the telephone. It had been years since Wash had heard from his Auntie Libby, who lived way down in swamp country beside the river, and he was surprised to hear her quavery voice.

'You in town, Auntie?' he asked, wondering what could have brought her out of the river bottoms. She almost never ventured out of her cypress house on stilts, down near Sundown Swamp. He listened anxiously as she fumbled for words. Her mind, always so sharp, seemed to be failing, now that she was ninety-three.

'Wash, they's talk down here. Yo' cousin Jimmie done told us somethin' big in the drug line is comin' in. He heard it from that Dooley boy, young

1

Wim. That boy, he knows just about everythin' goes on down here, and Jim told me he trusts his word.'

Wash could visualize his aunt's wrinkled face, now ashy in color rather than the rich mahogany he remembered from when he was younger. She would be frowning, trying to get every word just right. She hated what drugs had done to some of her great-grandchildren, and if she passed along the word, he knew it was probably true.

'Who's involved, Auntie?' Wash asked. 'And where are they heading?'

'Boy said they's comin' up the river to Boggy Slough. S'posed to meet somebody there to sell their shipment. Word was there's somethin' really important, too, but he couldn't find out what it was. You pass the word, Wash. We needs to catch all them drug pushers and put 'em in the jailhouse.' Her voice was almost gone now.

'You bet, Auntie. I'll pass the word to the DEA folks. It's not in my jurisdiction, being as I'm a police chief in Templeton, but they'll do the job. You rest easy. And thank you. Mama would be proud.'

He heard a sniff and knew she was remembering the niece she had reared from infancy. Good old Libby! Her heart was in the right place, every time.

The phone clicked in his ear, and Wash dialed the number he knew too well. 'Drug Enforcement Agency,' came the clipped response.

Wash passed on the information, knowing that the federal people really hadn't much use for local police. Sure enough, the girl on the phone was just short of rude, but she took down what he said. What happened now, Wash knew, was up to the agency.

If he had his way, he'd be waiting by the river a long way downstream from Boggy Slough, for the information network on the river and in the swamp country was formidable. If Wim Dooley could overhear something this important, somebody else could overhear the DEA's plans to catch the drug runners. You couldn't persuade the narcs of that, though. They seemed to think country people were stupid, which could be, in the wrong circumstances, a dangerous thing to do.

He hung up the phone and turned to Jewel. 'Let's hope those arrogant cusses do their job right,' he said. Then he went back out to finish hosing off the driveway.

Fifteen years ago, when he had just finished college and got a job on the Templeton police force, there hadn't been a black family in this neighborhood. Now there were three: his own, Dr. Ross's, and that of Samuel Trenton, who taught at the local university.

Wash didn't intend for anybody to point to his place and say, 'See? I told you black folks would mess up property, ruin the neighborhood and lower real estate values.'

The sun was down, but the sky still blazed rose and gold above the overhanging branches of cypress, oak, and sweet gum. It had been one of those days in east Texas, the temperature hot enough to wilt goat weeds and the humidity just about as high.

Sitting on his rickety porch, Possum Choa smiled. Folks in town were all sealed up in their houses with their air conditioners running, watching the nonsense that came over their television sets. Getting used to such sissified things was the ruination of people, Choa had decided back when he was younger and lived, for a while, in the same fashion.

He and his ancestors had dwelt comfortably in this swamp for centuries, putting up with heat, mosquitoes, and the lack of what others thought of as civilized entertainment. Even the water moccasins and alligators were interesting — though he avoided them wherever possible.

Every evening he had a concert all to himself, just about the time the sun began to set, sending slanting rays of fire down through rifts in the leaf-cover, when the little frogs began to sing. His Daddy told him they said: 'Ankle-deep! Ankle-deep!' Then katydids took up the melody, zee-zawing in the trees. Bigger frogs tuned up with: 'Knee-deep! Knee-deep!'

And finally the big old bullfrogs began roaring, 'Belly-deep! Belly-deep!' And things warmed up fast. Now the crickets and locusts were chirking and shirring and ticking all around him — over in the button-willows, overhead in the big red oaks that shaded his cabin, and out in his summer-cooked garden. Trying to pick out one song from the orchestra was beyond him; he listened to the total effect with contentment. He'd spent most of his life learning to appreciate such things.

An alien note crept into the chorus, and he cocked his grizzled head to listen. Far away, the sound muffled by intervening brush and trees, there was the throb of a motor. No road lay in that direction for twenty miles; it had to be a boat moving along the spring-fed creek that led from the swamp into the river.

What in the world was a boat doing on the creek at this time of year? In winter hunters sometimes came to jack-light deer that ranged along the low ridges, and game wardens came to catch them at it. In early summer fishermen set lines or illegal nets along the channel, and those same wardens eeled along after *them*. But in late summer, when it was this hot, there was nothing worth hunting, fishing, or trapping for that wasn't buried deep in the coolest parts of the woods or far down in the deeper water of the river.

There was no good reason for anyone to be there, that was certain.

Even the unusually big rains that had fallen earlier in the month couldn't explain that sound, for fishermen knew in this heat the big fish were downriver in the deep eddies, cooling off.

A grandpa bullfrog roared in the cattails at the end of the path. There Choa's boat landing staggered out over the murky water that turned, within a few yards, into swamp.

The multitude of croaks and creaks drowned out the sound of the engine.

Far overhead, a thin whine became a ripping sound as a jet shrieked overhead in less time than it took to think about it. For an instant there was silence as the choristers were stilled by the shock.

Into that quiet came the unmistakable sound of a yell, choked off almost instantly. Choa rose on tough bare feet and reached inside his front door for his shotgun. He took a box of shells from the ledge above his front steps, shuffled his dark-skinned feet into his tattered boots, and set off along the path leading toward the creek. Hanging on the trigger guard of his shotgun was a thong securing a battered flashlight, whose output just about rivaled that of two exhausted fireflies in a jar. He didn't use it, however. That was for examining anything he found. For travel in the swamp country, Possum Choa needed no more light than the occasional glint of a star through tree-crowns or the vague phosphorescence of rotting stumps and logs. His few acquaintances swore the old fellow could see in the dark, and they weren't far wrong. His nose and the air against his skin told him where he was and what areas to avoid, as much as his eyes did. His wide feet, booted or not, knew the trails through the maze of pools and runnels and sunken spots.

A screech owl shrilled overhead, and there were occasional rustles as snakes or small hunters scurried out of his way. Quiet as he was, the swamp at night was too crowded with life to allow him to pass without being noticed. The smell of the bog warned him to swing wide, following a deer trail up an almost imperceptible ridge and around a sinkhole's unplumbed depths.

Moving swiftly, Choa came to the edge of the creek and saw the line of reflected stars flickering along its middle. In moments the moon rose, red and warped as it waned. There were shadows on the creek, and voices muttered and cursed there. Sinking to his haunches, the half-breed strained to see and hear, knowing that his senses, trained acutely for sixty years, were sharper than those of people half his age.

The men in the boat were quarrelling softly, splashing unnecessarily with their paddles, and thumping their feet on the metal bottom of the craft to send hollow *blumps* through the water.

Noisy and stupid, Choa thought with disgust. What in hell were they doing out there? Tucked behind a huckleberry bush, a shadow among shadows, he gazed intently at the silhouetted shapes on the creek.

The boat was an old aluminum one; he could see reflections off the water rippling along its battered sides. There were three men in it, one in the stern holding a paddle as if to use it as a weapon, the other two strung along its length. The one in the bow was balancing a bundle on the edge. 'Here?' he asked, his voice sharp. 'Is this that special place you come fer to find, Oscar?'

'Keep your damn voice down. That yell you gave a while ago scared the crap out of me. And don't call out any names. You don't never know who's around, even out here in the middle of no place,' came the reply.

'Yes, there, you dumbass. Right under the bank — see the darker shadow there? There's a snag across the front, so if a flood comes, our stuff won't wash away.'

'I don't like this one little bit, Oscar . . . I don't like it at all,' said the small man in the middle of the boat.

'This stuff is pure gold,' continued the

one called Oscar, 'if we kin get it to our buyers. And the Big Feller said there's a bonus on this shipment, too. Somethin' extra hid down in the batch. Leavin' it out here is a bad idea. Anybody could come along and make off with it.'

There came an impatient snort from the huge man with the paddle. 'You think we're goin' to get any good out of it if we take it back and the narcs ketch us red-handed with it?' he asked. 'It's pure luck that Maxie got word to us before we come in to the meetin' place at Boggy Slough. Think of them narcs roostin' all around the slough,' he added. 'Mosquitoes eatin' 'em alive, waitin' for us to show up and get caught. Makes me laugh to think about it.' But he didn't sound as if he were laughing.

Choa nodded silently, understanding all too well who was invading his swamp. He had no use for drug dealers — or for narcs, either, if it came to the pure truth. No, he'd put a spoke in all their wheels, if he could find a way to do it.

While he watched, the moon tinged the treetops with reddish light. The boat crept close to the high bank and nudged its bow right up under it.

'You stick it up under the overhang,' Oscar said. 'Make sure the snag blocks it from floatin' out, no matter how high the water gets if there's a flood. And be careful where you put your hands. There's always moccasins in places like that.'

There came sucking and rustling sounds, and a sharp exclamation that told Choa the man, in spite of Oscar's warnings, had found a snake lurking in the water beneath the bank.

After a bit the boat backed away into the stream.

Then things got interesting.

Oscar raised the dripping paddle and brought it down on the middle man's skull with the sound of a hatchet hitting a ripe melon. The one in the bow looked back, but before he could dodge, the over-long arms, extended by the length of the heavy paddle, had split his head wide open too.

While Choa watched, Oscar carefully placed the two bodies in the same undercut hollow where the drugs had been hidden. It took him some time; maneuvering dead bodies in a small boat is usually a mighty awkward business, apt to get everything dumped overboard or the boat overturned. But he got it done at last. Then he turned the prow down-stream toward the river and began paddling silently, sliding through moon-light and shadow like an over-solid ghost.

Choa, knowing where he had to go, rose and ran along familiar paths that cut across the creek's meanderings to a point three miles down the creek where another overhanging bank would give him a good place to wait.

A creek bank at night is not a quiet spot. He could hear a gator bellow, the shriek of some small animal falling prey to a bigger one. A whippoorwill mourned among the trees, and a screech owl whimpered fretfully. There was a flop in the water where some late-feeding fish struck at a belated insect. Frogs croaked and crickets sang, different songs from those beside the cabin but familiar for all that. A hoot-owl called and another answered in the depths of the woods behind him, while a mockingbird struck up his middle-of-the-night solo.

The racket was so noisy that Choa almost missed the clunk of a paddle striking the side of the boat, just beyond the bend. Below and to his left, the craft slid into a puddle of moonlight, now riding high in the shallow water.

Choa raised his shotgun with great care, taking aim at the waterline. The blast of the shot sent birds squawking from the trees around him, silenced the crickets, and sank Oscar and the boat quickly into the shoulder-deep creek.

The night filled with lurid language, but Choa was already moving away, running as lightly as a boy along the hidden trails toward his cabin.

Nobody knew where he lived. Few even knew of his existence. So far from the site of Oscar's murders, the big man would have no idea who had sunk his boat, or why. He certainly wouldn't return tonight to check on his stash or his victims. Not on foot in swampy country that could swallow a man, even one of his size, without a burp.

Tomorrow, Possum Choa thought, he would attend to things himself. He didn't like having his swamp dirtied up with drugs and runners.

★   ★   ★

Morning found Choa in his own boat, made of a single cypress log by his father, pushing through cattails, waterweed, and muck on his way back to the creek to tidy up. He tied his craft to a willow some quarter-mile from the spot he wanted and moved along the bank, listening and watching.

Ironweed raised purple clusters in the few sunny spots, and brown and yellow butterflies rose from mud patches as he went down to the water beside the hole in the bank. He waded out into the tepid water, hip deep, shoulder deep, making for the dark patch that hid two bodies and a big cooler full of dope ... and something that might be even more valuable to townsmen.

He tapped against one of the oak roots that curved like teeth down over the washed-out niche, and two water moccasins slid away, giving him dirty looks as they swam past. Nasty brutes! They were the meanest-tempered snakes he knew.

Cautiously, he peered into the darkness. Sure enough, a pale blob dipped as the water stirred. Behind it another — the faces of Oscar's victims stared blindly at him as he examined them. They were familiar faces, too.

Choa watched those who messed around in his territory. He'd seen these two more than once, setting illegal nets, or fishing up mysterious parcels out of the big lake on the Nichayac River in the middle of the night. Bad ones, those two. His friend King Deport called them Ben and Yancy. Better off dead, he suspected, as he climbed out of the water and set off in search of a likely log.

A big old sweetgum had fallen in a storm two years past. By now its great branches were pulpy, easy to break off, big enough to carry a passenger, and not likely to sink too soon. He dragged two pieces as thick through as his body to the edge of the creek, where he supplied each with a passenger, laid endwise along the log, arms and legs trailing off on either side to stabilize the load. Those he set bobbing along the current toward the river, knowing that if they hung up on a bend down the way he could follow along and push them loose. While they made the first leg of their journey, he moved back into the woods and straightened up all sign of his passing.

The sweetgum log fell apart under his efforts, and there was no sign left that any branches were missing. Not that any agent of the law had bat sense when it came to reading sign in the woods; but Choa never left anything to chance.

When he was done, nobody but his pa or his grampa, both long dead, could have told anyone what had gone on there.

It took only a couple of pushes to get the bodies past the sharp bends and almost to the river. When he had that done, he went back to the hole and fished out the cooler, a big one, watertight, lashed with metal strapping and sealed with some kind of gunk. He put that into his own boat, once he brought it into position, and headed upstream into the swamp. There was an alligator hole there on another of the complex of creek branches that would just suit this cargo.

The gators were out in the water, keeping cool and watching for snacks of fish or water moccasins. The mud bank on which they rested stunk of them, and the hole of water there was deep. He heaved the heavy box over the side of the boat, knowing that the weight Oscar had put into it to hold it in place in the creek-bank would sink it here.

Sure enough, it went down, slowly but without hesitation, until it was just another lump in the mud ten feet below him. No bubbles marked its passing, which told him the thing was sealed even better than he thought.

Even if Oscar figured out where it was, which he'd never do in a million years, the idea of his trying to retrieve his stash under the eyes of a dozen eight- to ten-foot alligators was enough to send Choa home laughing fit to kill.

No, take it how you might, old Oscar was going to be in hot water when the bodies of his victims came rolling down the river on their logs. And when his big boss, whoever that might be, wanted the money for the drugs the three were supposed to deliver, not to mention whatever else the shipment held, that was going to make life interesting for him, too.

All in all, Possum Choa was well satisfied with his work. He'd know if anyone came looking through his swamp; he'd take a hand again, if there seemed any need for that. And if Oscar's body turned up someplace strange and hidden — well, that was all right, too.

2

Witch Stuff

Two days went by slowly, for it set in to rain again. It had been a mighty wet year already, and this downpour meant floods. Choa knew nobody would venture up the creek amid all the debris that was washing down the current, carried out of the swamp by the flood waters.

It rained buckets for days. The goatweeds perked up, and the frogs were delirious with joy. Only the water moccasins, taking refuge in button willows and his cape jasmine bush, seemed out of sorts, but they were always bad-tempered.

There was so much fresh food in the water that the fish weren't biting, but Choa managed to snare rabbits and raccoons that used his secret paths to avoid the high water. Nobody ever went hungry in the swamp. His Indian ancestors would have starved when their tribe was driven out of the upland woods by Spaniards and Anglos, if they hadn't known how to survive there. As it was, they retreated into the swamps, where no white man came, and managed very well.

From time to time a black slave had escaped from his or her masters and joined the growing clan amid the great gums and oaks and cypresses, and protected by the treacherous sinkholes, enriching the tribe with new blood and different skills and stories. All had settled in together, forming a tough amalgam of heritages.

It made Choa a bit lonely, thinking about those lost times when there were many of his kind. His grandfather had told him tales about it, though by the time Choa was a boy the group had dwindled to his immediate family.

When his brothers decided to go out into the world, it had saddened their parents, who were old by then. Only Choa had remained to care for them until they died. He had gone out then, himself, to work on the coast for a time, but he'd returned with his wife to their home country. It was just too crazy out in the white man's world.

He felt no sorrow for what was lost. It lived, still, in his memory and his store of his grandfather's stories. His only regret was that Lia, his cousin and wife, had not lived past middle age. A fever had taken her, and all his willow bark and bitter clover teas and snakeroot preparations did her no good. She raved and she died, and he buried her on a ridge in the pine forest north of the swamp. He still missed her, but he was used to that now.

Sitting on his stoop, barely sheltered from the persistent drizzle by the brush roof, he found himself unusually gloomy. When such moods came over him, he found some useful work.

The wild pig he had shot in the night would spoil if he didn't share the meat. It was impossible to smoke pork in such hot, damp weather, for it always spoiled. He had cleaned it early, and now the bloody chunks hung in his kitchen shed.

He would go to visit Miz Lena, in her ancient house in the McCarver woods, taking her a shoulder and some ribs. If she happened to mention wanting to do something in return — not otherwise — Choa would ask her to use her old-world skills to detect anyone moving through the swamp who had no business there.

Lena McCarver was a bit frightening, even to one as old and tough and knowing as Possum Choa, but there was no meanness in her. At least, not toward those who meant her no harm. They'd been friends, of a sort, for his whole life. Besides, he was fascinated by her ancient house, the huge brass-bound book that lived on her table, and the two dolls sitting on a shelf in her kitchen. The story she told about those dolls was a strange one, but somehow he believed it.

According to her, she'd transferred the spirits of two bank robbers who thought they'd hide out in her house, putting them into those dolls while she had used the men's bodies to cut her winter wood. After that she turned the pair over to the law and got a hefty reward, but those dolls were still spooky. There was still a strange tingle left in them that he got when he looked into their black button eyes. Somehow, they seemed to be alive — or at least to remember having been alive.

Choa packed up the pork in a wet burlap bag and wrapped that in a dry one. Then he set out along the path northward, shotgun in his left hand, bag over his shoulder, snake stick in his right hand.

The paths ran with water, but this time he was moving gently upward, and there were no sinkholes in this direction. He made good time, despite the mud, and eventually he came out of the edge of the swamp onto the damp leaves beneath tall oak and ash and hickory trees.

The walking was easier now, and he sped on, coming into the stand of immense pines that rose like columns, their toes rooted in soil so shaded that there was no undergrowth, only matted needles accumulated over decades. This was McCarver land, the timber standing as it had stood since old Lena's great-great-grandfather claimed it.

The McCarvers didn't sell land or timber. Even now that Lena was the last one left, she had no use for anything offered by the world beyond her woods and pastures. Choa, feeling just the same, was not puzzled by that, but he knew that others were.

When he came over the last tall ridge, he could see the roof of her old gray house rising, sharp-angled, from the tangle of crepe myrtles, privet, yaupon, and vines that all but swallowed the structure.

It was amazing to Choa that the place hadn't fallen down around the old lady's ears long ago, but something — maybe her iron determination — kept most of it upright and fairly dry. Of course, once she got that reward for the bank robbers she had fixed it up a bit, shoring up the floor and the roof in the part she inhabited.

Maybe ... He shook his head and sighed. Maybe there was more to her claim to be a witch than anyone credited, too. She had, you had to admit, caught those two bank robbers. For a little old woman to capture two big, mean ex-convicts took more than normal abilities.

He'd been watching from the ridge, of course, when the sheriff's people came to pick them up. Those two bruisers had been cowed. They'd kept themselves on the far sides of the deputies, trying to stay a maximum distance from Lena, as they were taken up her weedy path to the gate and the waiting cars.

He moved down the slope toward the hollow where the house waited, whistling to give her warning that company was coming. Like most solitary people in the big woods, she didn't like surprises. She did, however, appreciate company, if it didn't mean any upset to her habits.

He could see her white head bob into view at the end of the porch, just topping the overgrown nandina bush. She waved something blue — probably her apron — to encourage him to come on down.

Lena was a tiny old woman, skinny as a stick, with a knob of hair screwed so tight at the back of her head that it made the end of her pointed nose seem likely to punch through the skin. Her bright black eyes were sharp enough to see through walls, which he sometimes thought they might well do. Now they were beaming with pleasure.

'Possum, how you doing?' she asked in her cracked treble. 'Haven't seen you since spring when you brought me that monster catfish. I eat on him for a week, and the tomcat finished up the bones and the scraps.'

'Brought you some pork, Miz Lena. Killed a wild pig last night and thought you might like a bit. Course you'll have to eat it pretty fast. It'll spoil mighty soon, this kind of weather.' He offered her the bag, and she clasped it to her bosom.

'Possum, I got ways,' she said. 'I keep most any kind of meat, alive or dead, for as long as it suits me. You come on in the house and I'll cut the peach pie from yesterday and hot up some sassafras tea.'

They went into the kitchen, the ancient boards of the floor creaking painfully beneath Choa's heavier tread, though they only squeaked like mice under the feather weight of the woman.

The two dolls still sat on a shelf, staring out the tall window with shiny black button eyes. Choa shivered. Had she really witched those bank robbers' spirits into them? There seemed to be something left, some residue that made the rag faces look alive.

But Lena paid no attention to the dolls. She poked the coals in the wood stove, adding another layer to the heat of the day, and set her iron kettle on a back burner. 'It's warm already,' she said. 'Now set down and tell me what goes on down in the swampy country.'

Possum Choa sat warily in the splint chair. Setting his chipped teacup on the rickety table beside him, he took a bite of pie and savored it before beginning his tale. When the last crumb was gone, he set the cracked saucer beside the cup and began.

'A couple of nights ago I heard somethin' along the creek. Motor noise, a boat, a yell, an' I went to see. A man killed two others and put 'em in a hole with a big old cooler full of what I'm certain sure is dope. I sunk his boat, so he had to hoof it back down to the river, and then I took the bodies an' sent 'em after him, the next morning.'

The black eyes squinted at him over the rim of her cup. 'And what did you do with that cooler? And what might I do to help out?'

Choa grinned. 'Sunk it deep in an alligator hole. Figure they'll be lookin' for it, come a break in the weather. That's why I come to see you, Miz Lena. Think you can keep your feelers out for me? I know you got ways . . . '

The old woman sipped her tea daintily and set her cup aside. 'There be ways,' she said. 'I'll keep my ear cocked, you be certain of that. And if I find something, I'll shoot off Grampa's ten-gauge and hoist the flag on the big tree.'

Choa nodded. That old cannon could be heard for five miles in all directions. And her yellow banner could be seen all the way down to King Deport's place near the river.

Knowing that Lena was watching comforted him, for though he understood the swamp country better than anyone living, she understood other things from the old world. Though his own kind had myths and traditions of magic, hers seemed to include powers he hardly could believe to exist.

They visited for a bit, exchanging weather signs and conjectures about what winter might bring. Talk about the weather, in the big woods country, was not idle chatter but a matter of major concern to the few human beings living there. All of them were at the mercy of floods or tornadoes or forest fires in a way townsfolk were seldom aware of. A big flood could send everyone fleeing to high ground, a drought could deplete the supply of fish and game that kept most of them eating, or a drastic freeze in winter might well pinch the life out of some of the oldsters there. Big thicket houses were not built for warmth but for coolness. A wood fire in a rock fireplace or an iron stove was sometimes just not enough to keep the blood circulating.

'I see a bad winter,' Lena said, as they rose to put away their cups, preparatory to saying goodbye. 'It's been a harsh summer, and it's still hot as hell's outhouse, but the birds are beginning to go already, even before fall starts. The orchard orioles took off three days ago. The moss is thick on the trees, and I can feel big storms just pullin' themselves together in the north, ready to blast down on us.'

Choa shivered, thinking about it. His people had lived with searing heat for generations, but unusual cold struck clean to the bone, seemed as if. When the swamp froze, his tall-stilted cabin, whose walls were one pine-pole thick with finger-wide gaps between the logs, could work fine as an icebox. He was getting too old to sit on his stone hearth, with his knees in the fire and his backside freezing off. He said as much, too.

Lena cackled, bending double. 'Think I don't feel just the same?' she wheezed. 'My old bones ache fit to break in two, and my hands get so stiff I can hardly build my fire or cook on it when I get it going. No, Choa, bad winters ain't for old folks, but we have to survive 'em or go under. One of these days you'll come over that rise and find me stiff and stark in my rocker, dead as a pine knot.'

The half-breed grinned. 'If I don't go first, Miz Lena. It's got so I hate to see the leaves begin to turn or wake to hear the geese goin' over, headed south. But you gets what you gets, my daddy used to say, and I suppose we'll make do till our times come.'

She nodded and handed him a bag with interesting lumps and angles that made its sides bulge. 'Here's some sweet stuff. Got a notion to bake, when the weather cooled off with the rain. Got so many cookies and tarts and cakes I'm sick of the whole idea. Figured you might make room for my extras.'

He took the bag and nodded. This ritual was dear to both, for the exchange of gifts took place every time Choa came to visit. That only occurred perhaps twice in a year, but somehow Lena always knew and had a sack of goodies ready for him. Baked sweets delighted him, for he couldn't manage them on his fireplace, and he was no hand to bake, anyway.

As he trudged away, he felt those sharp

black eyes stuck like thumbtacks on his back until he topped the rise and started down toward the swamp.

He liked Lena McCarver, valued her as a friend and a practitioner of useful arts, but she scared the hell out of him, nevertheless.

$$\star \quad \star \quad \star$$

The rain had slacked off in the night, and by the time King Deport got himself out of his creaky bed and onto his even more creaky legs the water was going down fast. His house was on tall stilts, the floor well clear of even the highest water, so when he stumped onto his plank porch he could already look down into mud squirming with minnows, small perch, and a couple of moccasins that looked fat and happy.

A flood always made interesting things come to light along the creeks and around the swamp. King decided he'd take a turn through his domain to see what had been washed out of the sloughs and off the timber-grown ridges. He was getting too old for such things, he knew all too well, but as long as he could put one foot before the other he intended to keep a sharp watch on the land that his ancestor had been given by the king of Spain.

He boiled water and measured out coffee. Getting low, he thought. He'd have to get his nearest neighbor, the artist lady, to bring him some more when she went to town. Because her family acreage backed up to one of the big creeks feeding into the river, he could make it to and from her house without taking to the public ways. King avoided those (and the people who used them) with great thoroughness.

Irene didn't go to town often, though she owned a good car and had money for gasoline. She spent most of her time painting tiny pictures with watercolors or wandering through her woods or along the river, but she never minded bringing him things he needed. Never asked him to pay for them, either. Seemed she made a lot of money selling her paintings of the woods and plants and animals, though King thought that was just about the strangest thing he ever heard of. If money could be made by splashing paint onto paper, it seemed likely that every Tom, Dick, and Harry would be doing it instead of cutting logs in the woods or raising broiler chickens.

He gulped his coffee while sitting on the porch, dangling his calloused feet off the edge and spitting between the cracks from time to time to make the moccasins hiss with anger. He munched some cornpone for breakfast, washed it down with buttermilk, and dug out his boots.

It didn't do to go barefoot after a flood. You found snakes in the damnedest places, and moccasins weren't the worst you could get bit by. Coral snakes could kill you before you had time to think hard about dying. Copperheads were dangerous, too. He was too old to risk having to fight off snakebite, though when he was young a moccasin bite hardly made him sick. In the old days it just made him extra ornery for a week or so. That was one reason why he lived by himself, shunning other people. Once he'd killed a man, and it still bothered him to think about it.

He donned his boots, took his shotgun off its pegs over his iron cook stove, caught up his walking stick, and set off toward the river, watching where he stepped. The brush and grass were rippled by the action of the water, and drifts of debris were caught among them. The paths, when he followed them, were slippery and treacherous, so he kept his stick braced against any accident.

He followed his own private creek, which meandered through the forest he had preserved uncut for all his seventy years. In places the bank had been undercut and had fallen into the stream, but he knew from long experience that the water would soon find a way around the obstacle and continue toward the river.

The creek ran loudly between the sweetgums and pines on either side, its current far out of its banks. Yellow foam gathered around button willows and stumps; logs and branches were piled over just about every obstacle to its course. He moved clear of the creek and cut across a bend toward the river. He wanted to see what had come downstream from the bigger creeks.

Before he reached his goal he came to a knee-deep mudhole among post-oaks, where something darkened a spot on the far side. King was nothing if not curious. He grunted with weariness, but he persisted until he dragged his reluctant feet through the mud to examine his find.

Then he really did grunt.

A man's body, dressed in camouflage gear like hunters wore in the fall, lay sprawled in a tangle of saw vines and huckleberry bushes. The thing was swollen, its shirt split by internal pressures; its pants, tattered and ripped by passage through the flood, were only a sort of flap around its waist. The smell wasn't bad — yet — but it was going to be before very long. There was a crease down the middle of the skull, though the scalp wasn't broken. Just the bone. Somebody had hit that sucker a mean lick, that was for certain sure!

Damn! If he told Irene, she'd call in the law, and they'd tramp all over his land

and mess up his woods. While it had been years since he'd fed that pushy timber buyer to Grandpa Catfish in the big eddy, and there was no sign the fellow had ever set foot on Deport land, he'd just as soon that didn't happen.

No, he needed to send this corpse on its way down to the river. Nobody would ever know where it came from, if it made it far enough to be found. With the gators and the big gar on the prowl for meat, it wasn't likely it would be.

But King knew he wasn't able to do the job. No, he needed help, and the only one he could think of to help him was old Possum Choa, upstream in the swamp. That was a long hike, and it would take him a while. He'd better get moving . . .

He knew every shortcut, at least as well as Choa, and better than anyone else in the world. He kept going, though his joints protested worse and worse as he went. He kept clear of the lowest country, knowing it would still be submerged, or else hip-deep in gluey mud.

Making a swing up into the pine woods, he picked up a track. By damn, it was Possum's, or he'd gone blind and stupid. Seemed to be heading out of the swamp, toward the McCarver place. Sighing with relief, King propped himself against a stump, first checking to make sure some snake hadn't set up a prior claim, and leaned back to wait. If Possum had gone, then he was sure to come back, and this was the shortest way to the location of his cabin from old Lena's.

Maybe he'd have a sack of goodies when he appeared, too. King never tasted sweets unless he visited the McCarver house, and Lena wasn't as fond of him as she was of that black Indian. He didn't really blame her. When he was a boy he'd worried the life out of her and her mother. He'd even had the gall to ask her to marry him, knowing she would be insulted at the thought.

Witches didn't marry, she had told him all through their childhood. Witches witched. And nobody had ever known who her daddy was — or asked, if they valued their hides. Any man who'd gotten that close to Lena's mother had to have been a brave man or a damn fool.

He closed his eyes, leaned his head back against the damp pulp of the stump, and dozed in the sun.

Something bumped his toe, and he woke with a jerk. 'Possum?' He squinted at the dark shape looming against the glary sky. 'That you?'

There came a grunt in reply, and the man squatted beside him, laying a bulging bag between his knees. 'How'd you know I was out? And how'd you smell Miz Lena's bakin' from so far away?' Possum asked. 'I knowed you was sharp, old man, but I never thought you had a nose that good.'

King chuckled. 'I come to ask you a favor, Possum. I found somethin' along my creek that I need to send on downriver, but I've got so damn old and stove up that I can't manage it by myself. I need a younger man to help me.'

The bright black eyes blazed into his. 'Wouldn't be you found a dead man, now would it?' Possum asked.

King felt a shiver travel down his back. Indians had their ways, he knew, but he'd never known Possum to show much talent in that direction. 'How'd you know?' he asked. 'You didn't ... you didn't kill somebody, did you?'

Possum opened the mouth of the bag and let a tantalizing aroma drift out. 'Help yourself,' he said to King, 'and I'll tell you my tale while you eat.'

King stretched out his legs, set his straw hat at an angle to protect his face from the now blazing sun, and took a deep bite out of a fried apple tart. But as Possum's story unwound he found himself forgetting to chew.

'You mean you sent them bodies downstream, thinkin' they'd go all the way to the river, but it started in to rain and sidetracked one into my creek? That's sort of strange, when you think about it.'

'Seems that's what happened. And now I wonder where the other one is. I saw that man Oscar kill the both of 'em, and they sure as shootin' was dead when I put 'em onto those logs. I kind of hoped they'd get down where somebody would see 'em and start askin' awkward questions.'

He fumbled through the sack and came

out with a handful of chocolate chip cookies, took a big bite, and sat munching companionably as King digested his tale.

'Well, be that as it may,' the old man said at last, 'he's down there where he's no business bein', and I don't want no lawmen trompin' around my woods, scarin' the birds and all the little critters. Let's go get him out of there and send him on his way. Mebbe there'll be enough left, time the gators get through, to make some trouble for the folks that ought to suffer from it.'

Possum sighed and rose, reaching down a hand to help King onto his feet. He didn't insult him by offering an arm, King noted with satisfaction, but he did reach out to take the shotgun. That left both Deport's arms free to manage his walking stick and grab onto bushes and trees to keep his wayward legs from betraying him.

Together they trudged off through the pine woods, down the almost imperceptible slopes to the lowlands, and found the paths leading along ridges that rose beside the many creeks. They stopped to rest when King found himself tottering too badly; and every time, they ate more of Lena's provender.

By the time they came to the big mud puddle King remembered, he was feeling more energetic. The water had gone down even more now, and the body lay among the bushes with green flies making a frantic buzz about it. There was no sign of the log to which Possum had bound it, for the flood waters and floating debris had almost bared it to the skin.

'Nasty job,' Possum muttered. 'I never thought I'd have to do this twice!' He pulled the body across the mud and down to the side of the creek, where he rested it over a log that had floated in with the flood. 'Seems I ought to float it down this creek and heave it out into the river my own self. Still, that's risky. Might be some fool out there in a boat, just waitin' to see me do it.'

'We can go along the bank beside it and untangle it if it gets caught,' King said. His legs said otherwise, but he ignored them sternly.

'I ought to've done that in the

beginning, but I thought those two would hang up along the big creek and I could push 'em along the next morning. That rain caught me unawares; my bones didn't ache to give me warnin'.'

King nodded. Not often did his own rheumatism fail to tell him when weather was brewing, but this time a storm had ripped up out of the Gulf of Mexico and taken even the weathermen by surprise, according to what he heard on his battery radio.

They got the corpse onto another log, tied it with lengths of fishing line, and set it off again on its journey downstream.

'You go on back home,' Possum told King. 'I ought to've done it right the first time, and it's my job to do. I'll make certain sure it gets where it needs to go, this go around.'

Sighing with relief, King nodded. He watched until the log was out of sight down the creek and Possum was lost among the willows and gum trees. Then he turned and stumped his way back toward his stilt-legged cabin, thinking about bodies and how they seemed to turn up from time to time, no matter how clean you kept your nose. Well, this one was out of his way, and there would be no excuse for the sheriff to poke around on his land.

He found himself standing beside the big eddy where Grandpa Catfish lived. He thumped his stick against the ground, and bubbles began to rise. The big flat head drifted into view below the muddy water, and one large eye regarded him thoughtfully.

King reached into his pocket and pulled out a bundle, which he carried with him every time he ranged across his domain. Inside was a chunk of fat pork, which he flung into the water. The wide mouth opened, and the fatback disappeared. There was a concentric ring of ripples left on the surface, and the catfish was gone again. Just like the time he fed that bastard to it.

A hungry giant of a catfish was a handy thing to have around at times.

3

Out into the Light of Day

Possum Choa kept as far from his charge as possible, for as the afternoon grew even hotter the corpse became intolerable. When the log hung up on tangles of brush or temporary dams of floating logs and debris, he poked it free with a long pole he had cut from a hickory sapling. Even then he was nearer than he wanted to be.

The entire complex of creeks and marshes stank, in fact. After the flood, drowned bodies of small animals had floated to the surface, and the mud flats added their own peculiar taint to the mix. Choa was accustomed to smells of all kinds, but even he found the combination sickening.

All afternoon he kept after the bulky log and its load, which moved more and more slowly as the water ran down and the current slowed. At last he had to wade out into the water and push the thing ahead of him with his pole. But by sundown he was able to give a final heave and sigh with relief. The log bobbed out into the biggest creek running into the river. Below that point there were no more bends.

He ran along the bank, looking for logjams caused by the flood, but they had all been carried away downstream. From here on, that body could go no place but into the river. He didn't intend to let up now, though. Loggers had cut the timber near the creek's mouth and for some distance along the river itself, leaving a line of trees to stabilize the banks. Choa ducked into that and kept pace with the log, watching as it bobbed along more quickly in the stronger current that now had it in its grip.

Only when the sun was down and it was too dark to see did he leave off the pursuit and turn his weary steps toward the swamp and his cabin. He cut directly through the woods, knowing unerringly how to avoid low spots still sticky from the flood, and he came out just where he intended. He had left his log boat tied to a willow at the edge of the creek closest to the McCarver place. Now he got into the craft, loosed it from its tether, and paddled his way slowly through the darkness toward the swamp.

The moon was rising by the time he reached home. His bag of goodies was only a limp bundle now, for he and King had depleted its contents; but he made an early breakfast of sweets, drank about a pint of cold sassafras tea, and tumbled onto his cot, clothes and all. His catfish lines could wait; he was too old for this kind of nonsense, and he intended to sleep the clock around, if that was what it took.

When he opened his eyes again, the slant of the light told him it was after noon. The heat had glued his sweaty clothes to him. He struggled out of bed and ambled toward the pier to wash himself. Stripping off his clothing, he waded into the sun-warmed water and began splashing it onto his skin, scrubbing himself with twisted handfuls of cattail leaves.

He had just waded out again when he heard a roar from beyond his garden. Lena's shotgun! She'd heard or intuited something.

Refreshed by his long sleep and bath, Choa donned a clean pair of overalls over a khaki shirt. He pulled on his all-but-useless boots and set off for Lena's house. He left his boat at the pier, in case he had to sidetrack past King Deport's place before he returned.

When he came within hailing distance, he saw Lena on her porch, waving that blue apron again. She gestured for him to hurry, and he ran the last quarter-mile, arriving almost winded at her steps.

'The bodies you told me about? One of 'em got pulled ashore down at Samson Springs Marina. It was on the radio news. The sheriff and the federal boys seem to think it's connected with drugs.' She snickered knowingly before continuing. 'They say there was a falling-out among the drug runners, and the shipment they all been waitin' for might be hidden someplace in the river bottoms. What do you think about that?' Her shoe-button eyes were bright.

'I think they're most likely right,' Choa said, grinning. 'And they can look till their eyes pop right out of their skulls and never find hide nor hair of any drugs — not unless they're on good speaking terms with a whole passel of alligators.'

They laughed together, and Lena gestured for him to sit on her porch swing beside her.

'The only thing that bothers me is they'll go messin' around on old King's land — and that always upsets him something fierce,' she added, setting her teacup on her bony lap.

Possum Choa then told her of his adventures with King Deport the day before. She made a fine audience, chuckling and nodding at all the right places.

'But King's going to be powerful mad if they poke around his land or come to his house,' she said when he was done. 'Even if he did help set the thing off on its way.'

Choa agreed. He knew the old fellow

wouldn't welcome anyone coming around his land. 'Wasn't there talk a long time ago about some timber cruiser disappearin' down that way?' he asked Lena.

Lena peered at him over the rim of her cup, her black eyes shining. 'There was. But nobody ever found out where he went or what happened to him . . . and we don't want to know, do we?'

Choa felt a thud in his belly. Lena knew. But she would never tell anyone what it was she knew. She was protecting her old friend, and Choa had a sick feeling he knew where that timber man had gone.

'There's no way anybody could prove anything, though, is there?' he asked her. 'It's been too many years, and the body was never found.' He paused to scratch an ear. 'Old King — he never hurts nobody, and he helps when he can.'

'And we'll keep it that way,' she said, nodding. 'Nobody knows a thing, now, do they? Not even me. Nobody pays attention to an old woman in the woods anyway — or to an old Injun in the swamp; we both know that.'

He felt relieved. Lena was right. Those town people who sometimes tramped through the swamp and bottomlands, looking for this and that, thought they knew what they were doing, but they didn't.

No, King Deport was in no danger, but he was going to be almighty peeved at what was to come next.

★   ★   ★

King was already angry. He'd trudged, body tired and protesting, along the creek to Irene's back pasture. The four miles seemed like forty before he came in sight of her gray cypress house and its huddle of outbuildings. He scouted the place, as always, before venturing to go closer . . . and it was a good thing he did.

When he had worked around through the huckleberry bushes, pine trees, and saw vines north of her house, he counted three state patrol cars pulled up around her half-circle driveway.

Damn! He'd heard the news on the radio about the body being found earlier in the morning, but somehow he never thought they would come out this way to investigate. Didn't the idiots know that if you walked along the creek or used a boat, the road was no use to you at all?

He hid in a clump of bushes and watched until six men came out onto Irene's porch, their wide-brimmed hats in their hands, and headed for their cars. If they believed Irene Follett had a hand in this, they ought to talk to the sheriff. She wasn't about to have anything to do with drug dealers.

Only when the last sound of an engine had died away down the road toward the river did King rise and make his way to the back stoop of the old farmhouse. 'Irene!' he called softly. 'You there?'

There came a soft step along the wide central hallway, and her shadowy figure appeared behind the screen door.

'King? Sure. Come on in. My company's gone . . . as if you didn't know.'

She pushed the screen open and he sidled through, feeling uncomfortable within solid walls and an impervious tin roof.

'Come into the kitchen,' she said. 'I've got coffee on the boil. You might as well eat supper with me — I have green salad and cold pork roast and a peach pie.'

King felt saliva fill his mouth. If it wasn't for those two women, he'd never get real cooked food. Lena gave him oatmeal cookies, but Irene really *fed* him.

In ten minutes, he was filling his belly with her supper. Between bites, he asked: 'What did them state fellers want?'

'It seems that a body has washed down river, and they think it came from someplace in the bottoms below me. The head was bashed in, so they reckon it has something to do with drugs. Maybe so,' she added. 'But there are other things people kill each other over.'

'This time it was drugs,' King told her. 'I happen to know.' He held out his cup for a refill. 'A big fellow in a boat whacked two men over the head with an oar and hid 'em under a cut-bank. A friend of ours saw the whole thing. He's the one sent the bodies downriver.'

'So Possum was out and around, was he?' she asked. She poured him more coffee and sipped her own.

'Nothing much goes on down there that he doesn't know about,' King agreed.

Irene nodded slowly. 'That doesn't surprise me. Both of us keep track of each other, in our own ways. There are not enough of us down here — we can't spare a single one. And it makes me feel better,' she went on, 'to know he's keeping an eye on me. I'll do the same for him, as far as I can. If I hear anything that might affect him — or you — I'll get word to Lena McCarver. She'll let you know. I can hear that shotgun of hers clear up here, when the wind's right.'

They smiled at each other, reading thoughts better than words. People who lived almost entirely alone became good at understanding unspoken signals.

King knew they both hated the thought of lawmen poking around in the river bottoms, but even worse was the idea of drug dealers doing the same while looking for their stash of poison. The law might sometimes do unjust and unforgivable things to those they considered powerless, but dealers would kill you as quick as a wink and never think about it again. They were like alligators — all saw teeth and bite.

'You take care, Irene,' King said. 'Those are dangerous critters — both kinds are, in fact. They got no idea there's anythin' in the world but their own business, and folks like that do things without thinkin'. Lawmen are so set on gettin' the bad guys that sometimes they turn into bad guys their own selves and run all over innocent folks who get in their way.'

Irene gave a ladylike snicker. 'Ransome Cole is the exception. He's too lazy to pull up his own socks, as he proved both times I called him down here. I suppose with lawmen you either get the overly enthusiastic or the sluggardly.'

King thought a minute. He'd never had much to do with the sheriff, thanks be to God, but he knew all the gossip. 'Seems like he stays too busy keeping himself neat and clean and chasin' women to do much else. Might not be a bad thing, either. We might have him moochin' around down here more than we do, which would be almighty uncomfortable. Sheriffs best stay in their offices, where they belong.'

Irene looked him in the eye and grinned. Did she suspect his secret? Nobody had known where that timber man was going when he set out, and nobody had even thought to look around King's territory when he never came back to his employers and family.

Still, the thought made him uncomfortable enough to cut his visit short. 'I need some stuff when you go to town, Irene,' he told her, getting out his tally stick. She took down the items as he checked off the notches on the stick, and soon after, King Deport took off for home.

He went back a different route, wondering all the while if the state men intended to search the woods and the bottomlands. He knew they'd never tackle Possum Choa's huge swamp, but they could make themselves mighty unwelcome everywhere else.

As he moved quietly along a ridge, watching his feet to keep from slipping in the mud, he heard a distant call and a gunshot. Someone had found something, that was sure. Sounded as if it was downstream from the swamp, and he hoped it was nothing that would bring more intruders in, particularly dealers. They were pure poison.

★   ★   ★

Choa, too, had heard the gunshot, for his keen ears followed the noisy progress of those who searched along the creeks. Anything they found would have nothing to do with bodies or drugs, for he had covered the ground himself.

They seemed to have located the dead gar he'd seen beside the deep hole above Croaker Bend. It sounded like just about the right distance. Had they thought that long and stinking shape was another body? True, it was just over six feet long, but surely they could see the loose scales, hard as arrowheads, around it. Besides, it stunk like fish, not like man-flesh. There was a powerful difference.

He waded out of the edge of the swamp, pulling behind him a gunny-sack filled with mussels and cattail roots. He had a hankering for a mess of stew like his grandma made when he was a boy, and he figured to get the makings while he monitored the progress of the lawmen.

While his cook fire burned down to coals, he skinned the frog legs and cut them into chunks, peeled the cattail roots, and shelled out the mussels. All went into the pot along with water from his spring and onions from his garden. Then, leaving everything to simmer, he went out onto his porch again and cocked his hickory splint chair against the front wall. The sun was going down behind the western trees, and the shadow of the house stretched deeper and deeper toward the murky, weed-grown water.

A bull gator bellowed, and something splashed frantically along the river path, heading toward Choa's clearing. A mud-drabbled figure came into view, his hat drooping with damp, his boots slimed with green, and his gun obviously having been dropped into the muck. As Choa watched, he glanced up and spotted the cabin.

'Hey!' he yelled, breaking into a trot. 'Hey, you in the cabin! I'm lost! I need help!'

Choa got up and moved stiffly down his plank steps to meet the bedraggled deputy. Not one he had seen before, he thought.

The man halted and looked about him. 'You live way out here?' he asked, stunned. 'There's no road!' He stared around, looking for some access to the place by land, and Choa chuckled inwardly. Water leaves no track, and a careful man who wants no visitors and no truck with the outside world likes that route best.

'Don't need a road. Did I have a road, I'd need a car, and did I have a car, I'd have to buy gasoline and such for it. That'd take money, which I don't have and don't want. No, I just live here quiet and go about my business without any hassle . . . Name's Choa, by the way. Folks calls me Possum Choa,' he said.

A muddy hand reached for his own. 'I'm Larry Needham. I was helping out the Feds, searching, but I got lost. You live out here all by yourself?' He was still searching the clearing and the porch and the weedy garden patch for some sign of humanity.

'Since my wife died, I been by myself. Me'n the bullfrogs and that old dog under the house, if he's still alive. He's got so lazy he don't even wag his tail no more. You come in and get a drink of water and some stew. Got a pot of mussel stew just like my grandma used to make, about ready right now. It's near to dark, and you can't go wanderin' around. Likely to get snakebit.'

He hid his amusement as Needham washed himself in the water at the end of the pier, tried to clean his boots a bit, and laid his gun aside. They sat together on the edge of the porch, as Choa's table had fallen flat years before and he'd never seen a need to replace it.

The pot of stew sat on a couple of bricks between them, and they shoveled the food into chipped enamel saucepans, using half a hollow gourd for a dipper. Because he had company, Choa put out his two tin spoons.

The deputy seemed not to mind the crude utensils as he relished the stew and broke up cold cornpone into the gravy. As he licked the last drops from the spoon, he looked up at Choa. 'Peaceful out here,' he said, and yawned. 'I don't guess you got room for me to sleep the night . . . ?'

'If you don't mind the floor, I got some quilts to make a pallet. The bed we used all those years finally busted, so I just roll out a quilt wherever I happen to get took sleepy,' Choa replied.

From the snores that punctuated the night, Larry Needham had no problem with a pallet on the floor. Choa finally got up and took his out onto the porch, where the mosquitoes were no worse than they were inside, and it was a lot quieter.

Before the stars wheeled into their wee-hours position, he heard, very faintly, a human voice raised in a long call. Looking for his companion, he had no doubt. He smiled and turned over. Morning would do. No use to spoil the lawmen — might make 'em think they could come and go as they pleased in his swamp.

He woke his guest just after daylight. 'You want to get out before folks worry about you?' he asked. 'I 'spect we better get us a bit of cold stew and cornpone and be on our way.'

Groaning and muttering, Needham rose and staggered down to the pier to wash. When he returned by way of the privy, he was rather pale. 'You got a *snake* in that privy!' he said.

Choa nodded. 'Old king snake. I calls him Robby. He keeps the moccasins and copperheads out. I forgot to warn you — he's almighty big, and he looks scary, but he won't hurt you none.'

'Well if I hadn't been already sitting down over a hole, he'd have harmed my britches, I can tell you that,' the deputy replied, chewing on cornpone and taking a swig of spring water. 'You know, that Spanish moss you keep in there is even better than toilet paper. I'd never have believed it.'

'Folks used that before they was such a thing,' Choa said. He nodded toward the

pier and his boat. 'We better get movin'
now. Folks is going to be worried about
you.'

What he didn't say was that he wanted
Needham out of his place before anybody
else stumbled onto his home site. It was
pretty certain the deputy would never
find his way back, for he had no idea on
earth how he got there in the first place.

The boat rode low with two in it, but
Needham obeyed orders and sat still in
the bow while Choa paddled from the
stern, his strokes silent, his leaf-shaped
paddle never hitting the boat. 'What you
fellows lookin' for, anyway?' he asked as
he maneuvered the small craft around a
choked bend. 'I heard gunshots in the
evenin' before you got to my place.'

'You didn't hear it on the radio?' the
deputy asked.

'Got no radio. No electric. Batteries
costs money, and I got none of that.'

'A body came down the river, two days
ago, now. Pretty badly decomposed, but
somehow it had fallen onto a log, and the
flood must have flushed it out of the
woods along the river or one of the creeks

that empty into it. The man was a known drug runner, so the Feds figured there had to be drugs someplace. His head was all bashed in.'

Choa nodded thoughtfully. 'Sometimes I hear things from the folks I trades with. They mention drugs a lot. Seems to be a big problem in the towns now. What might drugs look like?' The question was quite sincere. He'd never seen anything druggier than a bottle of aspirin that King had given him once, after he'd been snakebit.

'Some is white powder. Some can be capsules of different kinds and colors. Marijuana is like dried herbs, I guess you'd say. This is probably cocaine, and that is usually either a powder or hard chunks. You keep an eye out for some kind of container with such stuff in it, and if you find it you get somebody to call the sheriff. There may be some kind of reward. We probably won't find it, if my experience here is any indication.'

Choa agreed completely. Even if someone had a 'visioning' like Miz Lena and foretold exactly where that container was, it wasn't likely there'd be any volunteers to dive there, right under the eyes of a half dozen large gators, and bring it up again. And if anyone shot an alligator, with the laws like they were, he'd be in big trouble.

The creeks ran into each other, around bits of higher ground, through choked woods, and wandered in deep loops. It was like a maze, and Choa felt sure Needham hadn't the skill to note landmarks. There was no way he'd ever find his way back again. Besides, Choa intended to block off that path he'd followed with clumps of button willow and huckleberry, so it looked as if there had never been a path there at all.

They found the big creek well before noon, and there were traces of the search on the banks and along the trails beside the water. Somebody had a good head, Choa decided, for they were searching under cut-banks and in deep eddies. Too bad he'd messed up things for them, though he wasn't *too* sorry. He'd heard tell that sometimes drugs got 'lost' with lawmen and turned up on the market anyway.

'You yell and see if anybody's left around here,' he said to his passenger. 'We'll go on down to the river, if need be, but I got things to do back home. My setlines need runnin'.'

Needham raised himself cautiously and cupped his hands about his mouth. 'Whooeee!' he shouted, the sound echoing back from the woods beyond the next bend.

Four times he yelled, and on the heels of the fourth they heard a pistol shot, cracking sharply through the muggy air.

'Sounds like somebody still hasn't give you up,' Choa said. He dug in with his paddle, and they moved downstream toward the source of the sound.

Another shot, nearer, told them that someone was coming fast. Choa pushed the prow of his boat against the bank and asked apologetically: 'You mind gettin' out here? I don't mix with folks hardly a'tall, and it makes me nervous. Just tell 'em old Possum brung you out. They'll know. I don't see folks much, but my friends tell me those that needs to knows my name.'

Needham stepped out onto the muddy bank, his weapon — still needing a good cleaning and oiling — in his hands. He shifted it around and stuck out his right hand to Choa. 'I thank you, Possum Choa. You just about saved my life last night, and I'm grateful. Anytime you need help, you send word. Don't forget my name. I'll do what I can for you.'

'I'll be sure to,' Choa said. 'Now you stay right here on the bank, and don't try to cut off any bends. This country, it'll fool you if you give it half a chance. Let those folks come up with you. You done enough walkin', I reckon, to do you a while.' He grinned and backed the boat off the mud.

Choa turned the bow upstream and dug in with his paddle, feeling the resistance of the current. He'd be well out of sight before the rescuers arrived, and if they came upstream to look for him — well, there were more creeks than one that emptied out of his swamp. If they picked the right one to follow, they deserved to catch up with him.

4

Questions! Questions!

It was late, already hot and steamy, when Lena got up, and the tomcat rubbing her ankles didn't help any.

'You got to wear that fur coat, Cat!' she grumbled. 'But don't try to share it with me. I'd take off my skin this morning, if I could.'

She hobbled into the kitchen barefoot and set her kettle on the range, punching up the ash-covered coals and sticking in some split wood. A wood-burning cook stove was nice in winter, but in summer it just added to the misery. However, hot mint tea always made her sweat, and that helped cool her off.

She was sitting on her porch swing, sipping her tea, when the sound of an approaching car made her prick up her ears. Lone, the tomcat, did the same, rising from his molten slump on the pine planks to sit on the steps and watch the road with narrowed green eyes.

'I don't like it, Lone,' she said. 'Coming on the heels of the news Possum brought me, it bodes no good. I'd better put on my dress before they come around the last bend. Don't want to shock anybody by being in my nightie at almost noon.'

She whipped into her bedroom and slipped a sleeveless cotton dress over her skimpy nightgown. Then poured another cup of tea, now strong enough to melt the enamel off her teeth, and stepped back onto the porch as a dusty Chevy bumped around the last bend and sighed to a stop beyond her rickety gate. She waved away the dust that drifted to her from the road and watched two men in uniform crawl out of the car and approach.

'Ma'am?' one called. 'Is it all right to come in?'

At least they were mannerly. Folks around here didn't like people barging into their yards without any invitation.

She nodded. 'Come on,' she said. 'We'll set on the porch. It's cooler out here.'

The taller man removed his hat and

gestured to his smaller and younger companion to do the same. He reached into his shirt pocket and brought out his identification. 'I'm Lieutenant Hardy, ma'am. This is Johnny Sanders.' He looked down at his notebook and asked, 'Are you Miz McCarver?' There he seemed to get stuck, his Adam's apple wobbling but no words coming out.

Lena grinned and nodded. She knew how she affected people who had never met her before. It had always been that way, after her grandmother had taken her in hand. Greatmom, they had called her, because she lived past one hundred years, and had all the knowledge in the world in her wizened fingertips.

Greatmom had looked at her sharply one day, when she was about five, then took her by the hand and led her down to the henhouse. There she had sat her down, right there amongst the biddies, and picked one up. Turning it on its back, she patiently showed young Lena how to 'stick' the bird — put it in a spell — just by staring straight into its eyes and crooning to it.

'You 'member how to do that, girl,' the old woman said. 'You 'member that and you can work your way with most anyone. You got the gift, girl,' she added. 'Don't you e'er forget it.'

'So,' Lena said this day to the lawman, after he'd cleared his throat and spat, 'what brings you fellers down here into the bottoms on such a hot day? Got anything to do with that body the radio's been talking about?'

'Yes, ma'am,' Hardy said, nodding. 'We're asking everyone down here if they've heard or seen something that might help us find who killed that man — and what they did with the drugs he and his partners were bringin' in.'

'Partners, eh?' she said. 'There wasn't any mention of that on the radio.'

'Oscar Parmelee was the ringleader of the bunch, and he's disappeared from his usual haunts. A runty little guy named Yancy Flynn usually ran with them. The only one we've found was Ben Falls, the one that floated down the river on that log.'

Lena frowned thoughtfully. She had no

intention of telling them anything she knew, but she tried to stay on the right side of the law. It came in handy, at times.

'I heard some calling and shooting last night, in the bottomland, close to the swamp,' she said. 'I figured it was you folks searching after somebody.'

Hardy nodded. 'One of our deputies got lost and we looked all night. An old fellow called Possum brought him out this morning, and then went back wherever he came from. You know anybody named Possum?'

She laughed. 'Possum Choa? Everybody knows who he is, but precious few have laid eyes on him. I see him maybe once or twice a year, when he trades me catfish and wild hog meat for stuff he can't grow in the swamp.'

'Do you know where he lives?'

She shook her head. 'Nobody knows where he lives. If your man found him, he must have been *considerable* lost.'

Hardy looked embarrassed. 'Our man tried to tell us how to get back there, but we couldn't find him.'

'And they won't,' she said. 'Choa's folks lived in this country before the white folks and the Cherokee came in. He may be the last of the old ones left. If he doesn't want to be found, you can bet he won't be. Possum doesn't like to be around people, particularly white people.'

'He ever have more money than you'd think he should?' piped up young Sanders. 'Or dress better than usual — anything like that?'

Lena bent double with laughter. When she could speak, she wiped her eyes and said: 'Son, if Choa ever had so much as a penny, since he quit working outside, I never heard about it. He doesn't hold with money, has no need for it, and wouldn't take it if you offered it to him. He gets what he needs from the swamp, and from trading along the creeks and the river.'

'You mean he never has *any* money?' the young man persisted.

'Not that I ever saw,' she replied. 'He dresses in whatever hand-me-downs folks can spare. When his old boots go to pieces, we chip in to buy him some more.

No, if Possum ever showed up in anything that didn't have more holes than a mudflat, we'd all pass out from shock.'

She could tell Sanders didn't believe a word of it. He was raised in town, where money measured a man's worth. A man without money just didn't exist; she could see that conviction in his eyes.

But Hardy was more down-to-earth. 'One of the old kind, is he? Self-sufficient and hard-headed?'

She nodded. 'Choa helps those he can help and never harms anybody that doesn't try to harm him. I've known him since he was born. But I wouldn't go out of my way to make him mad, if I was you. Messing around in his swamp is a good way to do that.'

The lieutenant looked away across the hill toward the swamp. His eyes narrowed, and Lena turned to look, too. A circle of buzzards was just visible above the trees that topped the hill.

She looked away. 'Might be there's another body out there that didn't wash down with the flood,' she suggested. 'You just might try to see what those critters are checking out, if you feel like a long walk.'

Hardy rose, and Sanders followed. 'We'll do that. Thank you, Miz McCarver, for your time.'

Lena watched them trudge away over the hill down which Possum Choa had come two days before. Only when Hardy's hat disappeared amid the pine saplings did she turn back to the house.

She focused her thoughts upon that circle of buzzards to the south. There would hardly be two bodies left undiscovered in the area, she felt certain. This had to be that Yancy fellow that Hardy and Sanders were looking for.

Knowing that King Deport and Choa would be wondering about this, she sighed deeply. 'Might as well send up the signal,' she told the cat. 'King'll look this way before dark. He always does, just to see if I've got any news he ought to know. Good thing he can see the top of my big tree from the knoll behind his house — he'd be cut off for sure if he couldn't.'

She opened her ancient wardrobe chest and took out a triangular yellow flag.

Then, followed by Lone the cat, she moved outside, up the slope opposite the one Hardy and Sanders had taken, and approached a pine that must have been eighty feet tall. Almost invisible, a double strand of dirty white line hung down its trunk, secured to a stub of branch.

She loosed the knot and threaded the yellow flag through its grommets onto the line; then she pulled one of the strands, and the thing went up as if the tree were a flagpole. It caught, from time to time, on the rough bark or a dead branch, but at last she had it clear of the needled crest. The breeze had picked up, and the yellow fabric stood straight out, flipping slightly and quite visible. King would be sure to see it, she thought, if the old fool remembered to check her signal tree.

He was getting past it, she thought, though he lacked a few years being as old as she. Some people, sad to say, lost their edge at entirely too young an age. At something all too near eighty, she was still going strong, thanks be to God, and she intended to stay that way.

★   ★   ★

The discovery of the second body set the law enforcement people to buzzing around the river-bottom country. They probed into the swamp as far as possible, but the water was still so high after the flood that they didn't do themselves much good — aside from making a lot of water moccasins angry.

Choa watched their efforts from the concealment of thickets or from one of his treetop perches. It was funny, he thought, that people hardly ever looked *up* when they were searching for things in the woods. His oversized imitation squirrel's-nest coverts looked completely natural to townsfolk, and nobody ever noticed them. Untidy bundles of twigs, old leaves, and other debris littered the treetops in most oak and hickory woods. Acorns and hickory nuts provided most of the squirrels' winter food stores, and those were their favorite places to nest. Choa created his own nests, large enough to hide his bony shape, and anchored to branches heavy enough to hold his weight. He'd watched a lot of things happen in the swamp country over the years while hidden in those coverts.

But it wasn't the lawmen whose efforts disturbed him, though he hated to have any outsider rummaging through his domain, scaring the birds and the small critters. No, he feared the others who might come searching for that chest of drugs — and whatever else it contained. If anyone representing the owners came, he intended to be on watch.

This was not the first time drug dealers had used the bottomlands and the edges of the swamp to hide their contraband. It was simply the first time their activities had involved Choa.

His work kept him busy much of the time, however. He had his garden to plant for fall onions and greens, the tomato vines he had cut above their roots, his collards and fall squash to set into the rich black soil. Choa worked for his food, and this was the time of year when, like the squirrels, he must secure his winter food supply.

Still, he managed to venture into the tangle of creeks every afternoon as long as the deputies and the narcs kept looking. He knew they would never probe the most remote creek bottoms, much less the deep eddy around the foot of the gators' favorite sunning spot. Yet he worried about that stuff down there. Would the ice chest begin to leak at last and poison the water with its contents? Choa refused to risk any of the critters, and he knew he must move it eventually, burying it perhaps, or burning it. Still, he didn't want to raise it until all chance of being interrupted by intruders was well past. It wouldn't fall into the wrong hands, if he could help it.

The law enforcement people gave up in a week or so, and the birds and the beasts settled again into their late summer rhythms.

For several days Choa kept to his cabin and garden and the swamp beyond his pier, working and gathering his winter supplies. He brought in whole cattail plants, for he used the fluff from the long brown heads to stuff his pillow, and the leaves to weave baskets to trade to his neighbors for luxuries. He dried the roots and pounded them into flour for part of his winter store.

Choa could not spare a lot of time to keep watch on the gator hole, but he knew those who might come wouldn't be quiet enough to avoid his attention. The crows had just about cawed themselves hoarse at the law enforcement people over the past month or so, and he knew they would not fail to warn the woods people of impending danger.

He visited King Deport, calling him from the edge of the woods to keep from invading the privacy of his house. When King told him about the lawmen questioning those living along the road, he nodded.

'Best to keep 'em out of the swamp,' he said. 'Though I hate for Miz Follette to be bothered.'

'Don't you worry about her none,' King said. 'She can hold her own with lawmen — and druggies, too.'

'And Miz Lena figured out where that body was before they located it. I'd have sworn it would go right on down the river when I left it to itself. Must have hung up pretty quick.' Choa considered a bit before continuing: 'I like that lady, but sometimes she does give me a shiver up my backbone. My folks's ways can be kind of scary at times, but hers makes my bones feel cold.'

'You see her make a sticky spell?' King spat into a bunch of ageratum, just budding into a fuzzy blue blossom.

'I've seen her stick birds and little critters, but I didn't know she could do people,' Choa said, feeling that familiar chill down his spine. 'Even those bank robbers — I figured she somehow tricked 'em. You mean she used that . . . '

King nodded and spat again. 'Me'n her goes back a long way. Never get crossways with her, Choa, that's the important thing.'

That conversation had given Choa something to think about beyond his immediate worries. In a way the idea of such things frightened him, for his people's mysteries dealt with real animals and plants and such, while Lena's seemed to pull in powers he didn't like to think about.

But he kept working, and his fall garden got planted, with turnip greens coming up and tomato vines beginning to bud again. One day he looked around and knew he had everything coming along that he could keep without its spoiling. It was time for his fall break in the endless labor of surviving in the swamp.

Again he visited the alligator hole, smelling the rank stink of the big creatures that lay, dappled by sun and shadow, watching everything that moved without seeming to. Those agate eyes looked sleepy, but he knew they missed nothing. Better guardians he couldn't imagine, and he turned his back on the place with confidence.

He needed to check with someone who had a radio, to see what was going on. If the law was done with the swamp, it was probably time for those on the other side to take their shot at finding the dope. He could either watch closely or rest, which he found himself needing to do; he had to know which was needed.

Although Lena had a radio, Choa felt uneasy about going back to her so soon, particularly since his skin was still crawling as he thought of people suspended by the force of her will. He'd always known Lena wasn't entirely safe to be around, but never before had that been so apparent.

He had never actually approached Irene Follette to talk to, though he understood she knew as much about him as he did about her. Now she had been questioned by the law, and he felt it was time for them to share information, and compare notes. It was time to close ranks again, he thought.

People who dealt in drugs in a big way were more dangerous than any alligator or coral snake in the swamp.

★ ★ ★

It had been the longest month Oscar Parmelee ever spent. Everything about that last drug deal had gone wrong, and now he had to wait and wait before he could clean up the mess. Every day he waited increased his own danger, he knew all too well.

It was strange that the Feds and the locals hadn't located the stash — and that was what worried him the most.

His contacts among the hired help along the river swore they'd probed under every cut-bank there was. Still, the one he'd chosen for a hiding place was remote, if you didn't know there was something to search for. Nevertheless, they should have found that ice chest, if the flood hadn't washed it away to hell and gone. If that had happened, and the unnamed but incredibly valuable addition the Man had put in with that shipment was gone . . . He shivered to think what might happen to him.

It might be on the bottom of the Gulf of Mexico right now. And then again, it might not. If not, he had to get it back, because the Man wanted either that or his money, and if he didn't get one or the other, Oscar knew his own hide was forfeit.

However, he had his escape route well planned, along with a supply of money to finance his getaway. Someone in his business who had half a brain took care of such things, but still he hoped he wouldn't have to leave. This was his home, and he wanted to stay where people knew to be scared of him. Breaking in new territory, with all the beating up and possible killing it took, was too much trouble, unless it was absolutely necessary.

He watched TV in his motel room, taking careful note of the progress of the different search parties. It was just bad luck, he reflected, those stiffs being floated out by the flood. But sometimes those were the breaks. If he just left things to rock along by themselves, and the Man got really riled, he'd probably join his partners in the graveyard, which was something he aimed to prevent.

Only when the media and his personal sources of information agreed that the last Fed had left the swampy country, did Oscar prepare to move. He didn't intend to go by way of the river, though. He hired a car under his carefully prepared alias, rented a boat and trailer, and prepared for a 'fishing trip.' He would go down Cottonwood Road to the boat launching spot on the Nichayac, get his boat into the water, and pretend to fish. He'd keep up the act all the way, until he found the outlet of the creek he wanted. There he'd find that stash, or he'd search out the reason why it had disappeared. Any fisherman who got in his way had better have his will all made out and his burial insurance paid up.

Oscar bought all the right stuff for a fishing trip: a white canvas hat with baits stuck around the band, a tackle box filled with bright plugs and fancy trout flies. He spent more than he intended, but he didn't dare steal what he needed and take a chance on getting caught.

He turned onto the oil-top road that became a gravel one and turned at last onto a rutted clay track, thinking hard about his goal.

As he passed the old farmhouse beside the road, he didn't notice the middle-aged woman sitting on her porch steps, half-concealed by wisteria vines, who took intense interest in his car, his boat, and his brand-new white canvas hat with the attached lures.

If he'd known who she was, he might have turned into her drive and blown her head off.

As it was, he zipped on down the oil-top, while Irene Follette nodded to herself and went into the house to find her keys. The drive to Lena McCarver's house was long, and at the end it got bumpy. The sooner she started, the sooner Lena could get the signal to Choa, down in the swamp. From his description of the big man who'd killed the drug runners, that just might be Oscar Parmelee who was headed down toward the river towing a rented boat and driving a rented car. That snow-white hat all but assured her of it. Every legitimate fisherman she'd ever known wore a stained, weathered, finger-marked hat. A brand-new fishing hat was something she had never seen in all her life.

That was no fisherman, whoever he was. Choa needed to check him out.

She pulled out of her drive and headed for the turnoff leading to the McCarver place. It looked like a cattle trail, but she turned off onto the cattle guard and bumped down the uneven track. Through the woods and across a shallow creek she drove, rounding the last curve to find Lena waiting for her at the gate.

'I felt like somebody'd be here this morning,' the old woman said. 'Come on in and tell me your news. I can see it sticking out all over you.'

'Get out your shotgun first,' Irene told her. 'I think Oscar Parmelee passed my house a half hour ago, heading for the river. Choa needs to know.'

5

The Sheriff

Sheriff Cole heard the ring with pleasure. It was about time he had one of these fancy cellular jobs, like the big city lawmen had. Grinning, he thumbed the 'on' button and said, 'Cole, here.'

'Well, Peanut. It's good to hear you.' The smooth voice sent a chill down his backbone. 'Seems like a long time since we talked,' the man added. 'How's Mae?'

Ransome Cole felt as if a snake had uncoiled in his gut. Since their earliest school days, Harland Fielding had been a pain in the butt, and that hadn't changed. The man had more money than Cole could account for and more power than seemed possible for a sharecropper's son from the backwoods — and there always seemed to be something slimy about his dealings.

'Mae's fine,' Cole said carefully. 'What

can I do for you, Harland?'

He felt a sick certainty this would have something to do with that mess down in the river bottoms, and he surely didn't want to get involved with that beyond supplying some deputies to help with the search. Missing drugs were pure poison, and a mess like this had put his predecessor out of office.

Sheriff Dolf McLean had made away with the evidence in a sting operation, and everybody, including the Feds and the highway patrol, knew just what he'd done. They'd caught old Dolf driving drunk, which had never been any big deal in the years before. This time they threw the book at him. Made him resign and took away his pension.

Cole had no intention of doing anything as stupid as McLean had done, but he had to keep Fielding happy. Nobody was completely clean, when it came down to it, and there were things he had done that Fielding knew about.

He shuddered. Blackmail was a nasty thing, when you were the one being gigged.

'So I'd like for you to take a *personal* interest in this thing, Ranse,' Fielding was saying. 'My friend has a stake in this, and he doesn't want his interests to be ignored, though obviously we can't go to the Feds with the problem. You just keep a sharp eye out for what goes on down in the bottomlands, and if anything else floats to the surface — well, you just glom onto it and let me know. Hear?'

Cole swallowed hard before answering. 'I'll see to it,' he said at last.

The phone clicked in his ear, and he suddenly hated his cell phone. It meant anybody could get at him, any time, any place. Not a comfortable thought.

He turned his car up the wide street to the courthouse, feeling his heart pounding. He breathed deeply, tried to relax, and finally felt the erratic thumping settle into something more regular and less frightening.

He glanced up into the mirror to see if his thinning hair was neat and his color had returned to normal. Had to look sharp for the TV reporters lurking around the courthouse, due to all the furore about those dead bodies. If he wanted to run for county judge next election, he had to look good all the time.

He punched the button for his home. 'Mae? You doing all right? Yep, I'm just going back to my office. Been down to check in with the fellows as they come in off the river. No, no more bodies. Got to go now . . . you take care, you hear?'

He hung up, worried. Mae was the one to watch over, with her emphysema and all. Never in a million years would he let Harland Fielding know that his wife was ailing. That would be a weak spot that Fielding would find some way to use, if the need came up.

Half a dozen men were waiting in the hall outside his office. Cole put on his lawman look and strode up the corridor, wincing at the sudden glare of a flash bulb. At least it wasn't the TV people.

'Mornin', gentlemen,' the federal official, Parker, said. 'Come on in. I've been down to the D.A.'s office, checking out what was found in the search.' He led the group, taking the only chair facing the desk, and waited for Cole to sit. Then he held out a computer printout. This was unusual. Ordinarily, the DEA people told the locals nothing at all, if they could manage it.

'Here's the report, up to the moment,' Parker continued. 'Our men have gone through that country down there, and I'd wager not a snake has been left undisturbed. We found no more bodies and absolutely no sign of any drugs hidden away. We can't spare the men or the time to keep on going over old territory, so we're turning the physical search back over to your office, Sheriff. The *drugs* will, of course, remain our jurisdiction,' he emphasized. 'If they are found . . . '

Cole looked pale and washed-out among the ruddy-faced deputies. But his steel gray eyes were hard and cold, and Ranse felt them stab into him like twin needles. Not a man to cross.

'I'll do the best I can, Mr. Parker,' he said. 'But if all your men and my deputies haven't found anything, it's pretty clear nobody else is going to, either.' He had a sudden thought. 'Did you catch sight of an old feller down there — he looks Indian but he's part black — living in the swamp? Possum Choa knows more about that country than anybody, if you can find him.'

Parker bent forward, his eyes bright. 'Why didn't you tell us about him before now?' The question had a vicious edge. 'Why didn't you pull him in for questioning? He might well be part of the drug bunch.'

Cole stared at the agent. He felt himself getting mad and did his best to control his anger. 'Mr. Parker,' he said evenly, 'Choa's people have been here since the Spanish rule. Never in over two hundred years have they given anybody an ounce of trouble. And nobody knows where he lives — better men than me have tried to find him to get him to show them the best fishing holes and such. Those who have so much as *talked* to him you could count on one hand and have fingers left over.

'He has no money, doesn't want it, and wouldn't do anything to *get* it. I've lived here, man and boy, for fifty years, and I've never seen him, though I grew up on tales about his family and later about him.

'He might have heard something or seen something — or he might not. And if he did, you could feed him to the gators, one leg at a time, and he'd never answer you if you asked him questions the way you just asked me.'

Cole felt better as Parker digested his words. The man didn't believe him, of course, because that kind couldn't imagine anybody that didn't worship money. But Parker knew *he* believed what he said, and that was good enough. The idiot couldn't find a big turtle in a small mud puddle — much less an Indian in a swamp.

After the Fed left, the other deputies leaned against the wall as if the starch had suddenly gone out of their backbones, and began to bitch about their past week's duty. Cole nodded judiciously and gave them all the rest of the day off. If he had to keep looking for a drug stash that probably was all the way out to sea by now, he'd find people who weren't tired to the bone. Then he got down to the paperwork he had neglected all week; but after a bit, he leaned his chair back against the wall and stared at the ceiling.

Harland Fielding was working for somebody who was deep into the drug trade — that was certain. And he wanted Ranse to secure those drugs for them, if any of his men stumbled across them. But if he did that, Cole knew he stood a good chance of losing everything he'd worked so hard to achieve. Dammit! And Mae was vulnerable. Without his salary and their medical coverage, he'd never be able to pay for her treatments. Yet, if he didn't do what Harland asked, he might lose his life, and Mae might well lose hers. That was his choice, and now he knew how it felt to be caught between a rock and a hard place.

Even if he could find some inconspicuous way of getting rid of Fielding, the Man who stood behind him was the real threat. Whoever he was, he must have informants planted all through the courthouse — and maybe even things like bugs in the telephone and computer systems that serviced the county.

Cole straightened his chair and stared

at his phone. Two could play at that game, he thought. He had a fellow in his jail who'd been caught in a federal operation aimed at finding computer hackers. That boy could do just about anything with one of those gizmos, he'd heard. Could he install something that could track down the information Cole needed? It was worth a try, he decided, whatever came of it. He picked up the phone and called the jailer.

'You got young Kramer in there still? Nobody's come and picked him up yet? Good. You just put him in the interview room and keep him till I get over there. I need to talk to that boy.'

He rose, hitched up his belt to settle his old-fashioned revolver on his hip, and stalked out of his office. Call him old-fashioned, would they? He was about to use *technology*, by God, to do what had to be done. Anybody into drugs big-time was probably using all kinds of computers and such to do his deals. If a slick and somewhat crooked kid could just tap into that network — whooee!

Grinning, Cole cranked his car and

headed toward the jail. Maybe things would work out, after all.

* * *

Agent Stephen Parker was ambitious. This drug case was no big deal, and was unlikely to make a name for the man who tracked down Parmelee and his cargo, but every little triumph added up. One day somebody further up the hierarchy might check his record and see that Stephen Parker left no stone unturned when it came to solving cases.

That was why Parker went to the county clerk's office after his last talk with the sheriff and got his own copy of the county map, with every dwelling marked and a key to the names of owners. Once he spread the thing out in his motel room, he found it hard to believe that human beings could bear to live in such isolated spots as some of those shown on the map.

He circled the swamp with a finger, trying to visualize the terrain again. It was a big area, and in the center of it there were no roads at all. Marsh was what the map indicated, and he'd been close enough to know it was right. Nobody could live in its middle, he was convinced. That meant that one of those houses marked as nearest to the low country had to belong to that Indian or to someone who knew how to find him.

'I'm going to take one last look around,' he said to Phil Voorhes, who shared his room. 'You get things settled up here so we can take off this afternoon. I'll make one more pass down those dirt roads and see what I can scare up.'

He had in his pocket photocopies of the reports filed by the deputies. As he proceeded, he checked off the houses whose occupants had been questioned before, comparing answers given him to those noted by the local lawmen.

Up one oil-top and down another he went, lining through names as he located the inhabitants, taking to dirt tracks whenever a marking showed a house there. Most of those were empty, with glassless windows staring blankly from gray walls, and sagging or fallen porch roofs. But he checked out every one, just in case.

At last he turned across a cattle-guard onto a crooked two-wheel trail through the woods that showed recent tire tracks. A car had been here not long ago, he could see, and there was a black dot that meant a house at its end.

He steered between great trees whose crowns loomed out of sight, making it dark beneath them. He had to go slowly or risk breaking an axle, but at last he came around a bend and found himself staring at an ancient gray house. One side of the roof showed a definite sag, and the other side was covered with corrugated aluminum, shining blindingly in the sunlight. A battered tomcat stared at him from the porch. Pots of geraniums and ivy, as well as flowering bushes around its edge, showed the gardener's touch.

Recalling the warning one of the deputies had given him about barging into yards unannounced, he tapped the car horn, three sharp, impatient hoots. In a moment the screen door opened and a tiny figure in a faded cotton dress moved to the steps.

'Who's that?' she yelled. He looked at the map. Lena McCarver was listed as owner of record. The second body had been found after deputies had visited her and had seen circling buzzards.

'Mrs. McCarver?' he called. 'I'm Stephen Parker, with the DEA. I'd like to talk to you a minute, if it's all right.'

'*Miss* McCarver,' came the reply. She made her way to the gate and looked him up and down. From her expression, he thought she wasn't overly impressed with him, but at last she nodded. 'On the porch,' she said, turning. 'Too hot out here in the sun.' She gestured toward a battered splint chair and took her place in an ancient swing. 'Now what can I do for you?' she asked. 'A couple of lawmen have already been here, when they located that last body. I couldn't tell them anything then, and I can't tell you any more now.'

It had been a long time since Parker had questioned someone he knew he couldn't bully. Now he looked into slanted black eyes set in a face lined by many years and a lot of weather — and felt doubt creep into his resolve. He leaned forward. 'Now, ma'am, I think you know just about everything that goes on down here. Do you know a man named Choa? I'd like to talk to him.'

'I been asked that, and my answer was just the same. I see Choa maybe twice a year. I don't know where he lives because it's so hid in the swamp that *nobody* can find it. What do you want with him, anyway?' she added suspiciously.

Parker chose his words carefully. 'The sheriff seemed to think this man might be a source of information about this drug deal — if I could find him.'

The black eyes grew sharper, peering straight into his. 'Choa's had no money since he worked outside,' she said. 'He needs no money any more than his ancestors did. If you think he'd deal with drug people for money, you're even dumber than you look.'

Parker narrowed his hazel eyes as threateningly as he dared, staring back into her black orbs. 'Withholding information from a federal official is . . . ' he began — but suddenly he found he couldn't speak.

Keeping her eyes focused on his, the old woman's hand lifted, fingers moving as if weaving a web. Parker's body rose to its feet and stepped off the porch onto the ground. Struggling to control it and completely unable to, he found he was being marched straight back toward his car, the woman following behind him, muttering under her breath.

They came to the gate and she manipulated his hands and legs to open the door and work him into the car. 'Don't think to sneak back out here and arrest me,' she said in a conversational tone. 'The owls watch for me. The tomcat tells me. The crows and hawks cry out to warn me. You can't sneak up on me, Mr. Parker. Next time I see you, I'm liable to march you out into the swamp until you sink in the muck for good. Keep that in mind. Now drive!' She clapped her hands loudly.

Suddenly he found himself in control of his own body again. He put his hand on the door handle to reopen it, but instantly it froze in place, and again he could not move.

Lena McCarver came to the car window and peered into his eyes. 'You're not in town now, boy. You're not in your office, wherever it is, with all the other fools who think they know the real world. This is *my* real world, and I'm the boss here. Remember that.' She straightened and pointed back down the road. 'Now get, before I do something we're both going to regret.'

He found himself driving along the shadowy track, feeling as if the trees themselves were staring down at him with contempt. He heard a shrill *skree* high above, and he thought about her words. *The hawks cry out to warn me . . .*

He put his foot down and sped around the bends at reckless speed, kicking up a storm of dust behind his wheels. He realized suddenly that he was perfectly satisfied to leave this case in the hands of the local sheriff — permanently.

When he returned to the motel, one of the local deputies was there, talking with Voorhes. Parker greeted the two men, saying nothing about what had just happened. But he couldn't resist asking about the old woman down in the woods.

'Philips, do you know an old woman named McCarver? Lives way down toward the river in a house that's nothing more than a shack.'

Philips shot a sharp glance at him. 'You been down there? My Gawd, man, that old lady scares the socks off people. I wouldn't visit her unless I had to.'

Parker shook his head. 'There's something odd about her, I'll admit, but what on earth could she do to anyone?'

'Well,' Philips drawled, 'she single-handedly caught a couple of bank robbers some years back.'

Parker felt a cold shiver down his spine. 'Then a cousin of mine swore he was going to sneak some logs out of her woods. Took a couple of his cronies with him . . . and not one of them has ever been seen or heard of since. His family didn't look very hard for him . . .'

Philips looked at his watch and rose. 'Got to get back to work. I just wanted to tell you goodbye. I don't 'spect we'll find those drugs — or Parmelee, either. Just a word to the wise,' he added. 'This county has been run by big money for a couple hundred years. The sheriff isn't a bad fellow, but there *are* strings tied to him. You can bet on it. Every public official in this county, with the exception of Washington Shipp, the police chief, has an invisible halter around his neck, controlled by the old families with money. They'd like to halter Shipp, too . . . but he'd die first.' Philips paused. 'And if you tell anybody I said that, I'll deny it with my dying breath!'

Parker sighed. He was ready to get back to his office, where he wouldn't have to worry about crazy old ladies — or corrupt officials who might hide things from him. This place was past history, as far as he was concerned.

He and Voorhes loaded their luggage into the car and headed north, both silent and thinking hard. Just before they got to the interstate, Parker picked up his cell phone and spoke to his superior.

'There may be a corruption problem in Templeton — and the county, too,' he told Davidson. 'We might need to check it out.'

'So what else is new?' Davidson drawled. 'Every little town in Texas has crooked cops and sheriffs and judges and police. You know that, Steve. You sound odd — what's happened?'

Parker shuddered. He had no intention of telling anyone about the incident at Lena McCarver's house. He didn't want people thinking he had lost his mind. No, let some other idiot snoop around in the swamp country. Crooked lawmen he could deal with, but crazy old women with eyes that stopped you cold and made you march to their beat were something else again.

'No, sir,' he said. 'We're on our way back to the office. I'm ready to dictate my report while we drive.' He touched the off button and looked over at his companion.

'Step on it, Phil,' he said. 'I really would like to get home tonight.' And that was no lie. Yet something inside told him he would have to come back — whether or not he wanted to.

6

The Watcher

Wim Dooley did his best never to be seen at all, and he had a shrewd idea he'd gotten so good at it that he might even beat Possum Choa on his own ground. Indeed, the boy had been practicing all summer, doing that very thing. He had watched Choa sit on his porch, run his trotlines, dig his edible roots and tend his garden. He figured he was the only person who could find Choa's cabin every time he looked for it.

But it was a shame he hadn't been down in the swamp when those drug runners were there. Wim would have bet his life that Choa had been paying attention and knew just what happened.

His ma didn't know a thing, of course. She spent her time working in the garden, boiling washpots of dirty clothes and chasing after the little kids, which kept her so busy she hadn't any time to check on twelve-year-old Wim's whereabouts when school was out. As long as he brought in stringers of fat perch or meat in the form of raccoon, squirrel, possum, or armadillo, she was content to let him roam. It took that much of the responsibility for feeding the younger ones off her shoulders.

But Wim paid close attention when the deputies and federal men had come around to ask her questions. Especially that feller Parker. He'd snooped around the place, rummaging in the woodshed, checking the ground in the garden as if expecting to find the drugs buried there, though it was plain that summer heat had killed most of the plants, and the ground was baked hard.

Parker never once asked the children anything at all. Even when Wim got right up in his face, all he did was grunt irritably and push the boy aside. He wasn't near as smart as he looked, that was for damn sure.

Why didn't he ask about where Choa lived? Nobody knew but Wim, and now he wouldn't tell that man anything, no matter what. There wasn't another soul he knew of who could find that cabin in the swamp, and it made the boy chuckle to realize that Parker had thrown away his chance. Not that Wim would have told him, anyway. Possum Choa was a lot better man than Parker, any day of the week, and Wim had no intention of giving away any of his secrets.

Today the boy slipped back through the woods, along the big creek, and upstream to the edge of the marsh. As he went, he checked his own set-lines, which were hidden beneath drooping screens of willows growing on the bits of mud-flat along the way. When he saw bobbing motions that weren't caused by the wind, he waded into the tangle and found his line, usually with a fat catfish attached.

He strung his catch onto pieces of line attached to low-lying snags of button willows. Those wouldn't move with the tugging of the captives, tempting others to harvest his catch, and he could retrieve them, one by one, as he returned home.

Before long he reached the swamp,

secure in the knowledge the family would eat well that night. As he neared the complex of streams and marshes forming the swamp itself, he moved cautiously. You never knew who or what might be poking around down there. His leathery feet, bare in spite of the water moccasins, found their way along paths he had traced and memorized long before.

When he came to the big sinkhole, he gave it a wide berth and slipped up the biggest of the creeks beyond it, ducking low behind the willows and cattails fringing the water. Although crows cawed noisily overhead, he had a feeling they weren't talking about him.

Somebody else was abroad in the bottomlands.

Wim crept along, almost holding his breath, until he came to the big eddy that formed the largest alligator hole. When he peered through the screen of brush, there was a log boat bobbing on the water. The gators on the mud bank flanking the hole were beginning to stir, opening and closing their jaws, hissing, and rising to waddle down to the creek.

That was Choa's boat! What was he doing there, practically in the jaws of the gators?

Making a quick decision, Wim rose to his feet, thrashed the brush with a stick, and squealed like a pig. The gator closest to the stream turned to face this new intruder, and Wim retreated, still thrashing and grunting. A wild pig in trouble would draw the gators away, he knew.

When he came to a huge willow, stout enough to hold his weight, he went up it like a squirrel. Nobody could outrun a gator on land, not for long. Here he would be safe until Choa emerged and found him, which Wim knew he would do.

Below him, three of the creatures rolled up their eyeballs to see him. Two females were accompanied by a bull that must have measured twelve feet long, at least. Wim grasped the nearest branches even tighter, sweating, not altogether because of the fall heat.

He heard a distant splashing and the thud of something dropping into the hollowed log boat. Choa was out of the water with whatever he had been diving for. Wim yelled as loudly as he could: 'Possum Choa! Help!'

The woods went silent. The gators didn't even blink, but in the distance another crow flew, cawing all the way. Then there was the sound of the prow hitting the mud bank, and a great hissing and shifting of big bodies as something moved through them toward his perch in the tree.

A sun-darkened face pushed through the willow fronds, ducked under a heavy branch of willow oak, and Choa began to grin. 'Young William Dooley, I'll be damned. What you doing up there in that tree, boy?'

Wim watched in fascinated horror as the old man kicked the big bull gator in the side. It grunted, whirled faster than anyone ignorant of the creatures' natures would have believed, and stopped. Choa was making a strange sound deep in his throat. It made even Wim's skin crawl, and it seemed to affect the alligators even worse. They turned, trundling back toward the mud bank, hissing.

'How'd you *do* that?' Wim asked, dropping from the tree to land at Choa's feet.

'My folks was dealing with gators when yours was back in Ireland fightin' Romans,' Choa said.

'How you know about *Romans*?' the boy asked. He'd only heard of them at school, though he figured that any people who'd been gone for thousands of years couldn't be of much use to anybody.

'I used to read books, back when I worked outside,' the man said. 'Learned about a lot more than Romans. But when I decided to quit being civilized, I quit all the way.' He looked Wim up and down. 'Now tell me why you're perched up there.'

'Well, I was sort of moseying through the woods, and I seen your boat. No sign of you, and the gators was beginnin' to move toward the water. Seemed as if I needed to do somethin' to keep 'em off you, so I began making noise to lead them away from the water.' Once the words were out, Wim began to shiver in dread. What had possessed him to do such a thing?

Choa shook his grizzled head. 'I thank you for the thought, but remember, boy, you never have to protect old Choa. Not in this country. Now, if ever I get in trouble in town, *then* I 'spect you might help me.' He looked at the boy, narrow-eyed before adding: 'What did you see, boy?'

Wim blinked, then decided the truth was his best option. 'Just the boat, Choa. Not even you. Though I 'spect you pulled up something, 'cause I heard it drop into the boat. I *guessed* it might be somethin' them drug runners left, maybe.'

Choa nodded thoughtfully. 'You guess pretty good, young Wim. So I might as well get some help, which I've needed and haven't had. You want to help me hide that stuff so nobody ever finds it again? I was afraid it might leak and poison the creek — so I knew I had to move it. Besides,' he added, 'I just got word from them ladies in the uplands that one of the runners is back on the river, probably tryin' to find it. It's time it went where 'nobody can ever get at it.'

'What about givin' it to the law?' Wim asked. 'That might be a good way to get rid of it.'

'If you'd seen as many lawmen down here doing bad things as I have, you wouldn't say that. I don't trust them any better than the runners.'

Wim had to admit Choa was probably right. More than one deputy had shook down the pushers, right there on the river. He had watched from the woods as a lot of wrong things went on. He nodded. 'Be glad to help you,' he said. 'Where you want to put it?'

Choa turned and led the lad through the huddle of gators and down to the log boat. In its middle was a muddy lump that looked like an aluminum ice chest. Choa gestured for him to climb over it to the other end of the narrow craft, and when Wim was seated, Choa stepped into his end and pushed off from the mud bank.

'I'm gonna put it in the big sinkhole,' he said.

Wim felt himself turn pale. He

swallowed hard before he said, 'No wonder you need help, Choa. You could disappear into that muck and never come out again.'

'That's why I want you on the end of a rope cinched around a good-sized tree. If I slip and go in, I want something to hold onto to pull myself out — and somebody to go for help if the rope breaks.'

That made good sense. Wim sat still, watching the alligators watch the boat as it slid out into the current and moved around the bend between fern-lined banks. At times the creek was so shallow he got out and helped Choa squish through the mud to carry it to the next navigable length.

When they were unable to go any further, Choa pulled the boat into a mass of cattails and they lifted out the chest, carrying it between them along the maze of passable paths that old Possum Choa followed without looking, no matter how overgrown and water-covered they were.

They came to the big hole just after noon, when the sun was high above the giant water oaks and cypresses that marched out into the morass. It was steamy hot, and the breath of the sinkhole was sour and stagnant.

Wim found his heart pounding as he helped Choa load the chest onto a small raft cobbled together out of dead branches fallen from the trees above.

Choa left him to guard their burden and went off to rummage around among the big hickories growing along a low ridge east of the hole. When he returned, he carried a long section of bark some three feet wide, slipped from a dead tree. Wim began to guess how he hoped to get out into the muck without sinking.

With considerable shifting and grunting, they positioned the chest on its raft beside Choa's bark. Then the old fellow lay flat on the bark while Wim tied the raft to it, freeing Choa's hands to paddle through the shallow water slicking the surface of the sinkhole.

Choa wound a thin rope around his waist and wrapped the other end twice around the biggest water oak. Once the strange craft moved out onto the muck, Wim stepped back and grabbed the end of the rope, while the coils of slack unwound slowly behind Possum Choa.

Fragments of bark shredded off to float around him, and the raft holding the ice chest began to tilt, bit by bit, as the contraption got out into the middle of the sinkhole. The hole itself was at least fifty feet across, although its edges were concealed by the bushes and vines and water-weeds surrounding it.

The last of the rope slack stretched straight, and Choa fumbled to free the raft. It tilted more and more, until finally the ice chest settled sideways into the murky mix of water and quicksand.

Wim watched, fascinated, as the muddy silver box disappeared with a glubbing sound and a bubble rose, to pop when it reached the surface.

Now he pulled on the rope, as Choa cautiously turned his slab of bark and paddled for the firm ground by the tree roots. Under him, the bark began breaking apart, and before he was within reach of safety it sank beneath the surface.

Choa grabbed hold of the rope, and

Wim pulled desperately, cursing the friction of the oak tree bark, which slowed his intake on the line.

'Just hold on,' Choa grunted, grabbing the line further up and beginning to pull himself in, hand over hand. 'You doin' fine, young Wim. Just don't let this sucker loose!'

Wim Dooley shut his eyes and held tight, though his hands, calloused as they were, began to feel skinned raw. Then he felt a touch at his knee, and Choa was there — covered with slime and mud — but grinning his wide white grin.

'Whoosh!' the boy sighed and sank to sit beside him on the damp leaves beneath the tree.

'I do say *whoosh* myself,' said Choa. 'I surely do.'

They grinned at each other as they caught their breath and rested.

'You going on home now?' the old man asked after a bit. 'I got to get on my way, too, because I've got things to do besides mess with this garbage. That man Parmelee's in my swamp, they tell me, and I need to see to him. *Nobody's* going to get their hands on that junk in the sinkhole any more, not drug dealers and not deputies who'd sell it back to other dealers.'

Wim nodded. 'I've got some fish tethered along the way. Better get to 'em before somebody else gets 'em. There's more thieves out there now than there used to be, don't you think?'

Choa grunted and rose. 'More everything bad than there used to be. The few of us that tries to keep things going down here better stick together.'

Wim thought about what he had experienced that day as he went home, gathering his stringer of fish along the way. He agreed with the old man. His ambition to take Choa's place, when he could, looked better and better all the time.

★ ★ ★

It was hot as hell when Oscar Parmelee got to the boat ramp in the woods. This wasn't one of the fancy concrete ones like they had at the state parks, but a muddy incline at a low spot in the river bank, and he almost got stuck backing the boat trailer down to the water.

Parmelee could see a dark green boat half-concealed by a screen of willows; the wide-hatted shape in it seemed to be running trotlines on the slough that angled into the other side of the river. The occasional slap and thump of a catfish dropping into the bottom of the boat was unmistakable. Nobody else was in view, though there was an old pickup backed into the bushes beside a tattered canvas tent, where a pile of ashes marked the site of a campfire. A cracked mirror hung on a nail driven into a hickory tree, and a washpan sat on a stump.

Someone had been camping here for a while, and Parmelee made a mental note to check out who was there when he returned from his task. However, right now he had work to do. He slid his boat into the water, checking the bindings of his gear as he secured the craft to the scarred sweetgum tree that many others had used for the same purpose. Then he hopped into his own pickup and followed a dim track that disappeared into bushes and big trees at the top of a heavily wooded ridge flanking the river.

The woods along the ridge were filled with mosquitoes and water moccasins in almost equal parts, and it was plain that few ventured there, except during hunting season. Parmelee nosed through overgrown clumps of huckleberry and yaupon until he found the sort of smaller track he was looking for. Backing the pickup into that, he locked it, zipped the key into the inside pocket of his money-belt, and rearranged the disturbed branches. No one would never know there was a vehicle there, when he was done.

He went back to the boat, got in and cast off, paddling off downstream toward the creek where he had stashed the ice chest. If it was still there, he would retrieve it, or die trying. But he had to avoid suspicion, and once he got downriver, he began to notice a few people about, some fishing with cane poles from the bank, another in a boat checking trotlines.

He looked for a quiet spot to set out a

line himself — just to keep up appearances. Around a bend, he found an eddy deep enough for bass, and attached his line to a red and white plug. He made an awkward cast into the middle of the wide spot.

As he slowly reeled in his line, he happened to glance up. There, hunkered down among the cattails and button willows on the far bank, was an old man watching him, who nodded slowly before returning his gaze to the river.

Parmelee cleared his throat. It was better to seem natural than stand-offish. 'Pretty hot for fish,' he commented. 'But you've got to take the chance when you have time off. Any bass in that hole?'

The old fellow looked up, and Parmelee was struck by the steely quality of his eyes as he gave another slow nod. 'Seen some big 'uns come out of that hole,' the man said. 'But you're not goin' to do much good today. Too hot. You might get lucky when the wind shifts tomorrow, particularly if it starts to rain,' he added. That seemed to be his limit of conversation, for he suddenly slid backward and disappeared — as silently as any Indian.

Was *that* old Choa that people had talked about for so many years? But surely it couldn't be. This man was white-skinned under his tan, and his eyes were so pale they seemed colorless. It couldn't be Choa, Parmelee decided. But it had to be one of the few people who lived here full-time.

It could be Satter Dooley's pa — but no, Satter had said that his pa died back around 1989. Then there'd been talk about old King Deport — but he'd be older than sin by now.

Still, this man *might* be King Deport.

But what would he be doing out on the river bank where folks were fishin', when everybody knew he didn't associate with people? It was unlikely King Deport would come down to chat with the fishermen.

Reeling in the last of his line, Oscar laid his rod in the bottom of the boat and took up the paddle again. There was nobody in sight now; he'd best make time while he had the chance.

The sluggish current was no help as he moved downstream, and he went too slowly for his taste, feeling as if some hidden watcher might be staring at his back. Although he passed no more fishermen further downriver, it took longer than he liked to find the tributary that would lead him to the creek he was seeking.

By the time he turned off into the narrow creek mouth, it was near sundown, and he knew he'd never find it again in the dark. The flood had changed the contours of the creek, as well as bringing down trees from its banks. You'd never know there'd been high water now, he thought as he pulled his fiberglass boat up onto a low bank and prepared to camp.

Talc-like dust rose around him in a cloud, making him sneeze. Might as well leave the boat here tomorrow, he realized, for already the creek was too low for easy boating, and it was faster to walk the bank than to carry the boat over the shallows.

Though he had been raised along the

river, Oscar had scorned the swamp life early and moved away to town. He remembered a lot of things and a lot of places, of course, but now the easy familiarity his father and cousins had with the critters that lived there had deserted him.

He put up his little tent, built a skimpy fire to heat water for instant coffee, and chewed on cold canned pork and beans. This wasn't the way he wanted to live. That was why he had taken up drug running — it was the only way he'd ever found to make a lot of money fast. But the big Man sitting at the top of the heap who never took a chance raked in the big bucks, while Oscar Parmelee sat on a creek bank and swatted mosquitoes. And if he didn't locate that missing stash, of course, he'd have worse things than mosquitoes to worry about. That same Man at the top had ways of punishing those who didn't deliver the goods.

He zipped himself into his tent, knowing full well that any black bear or cougar wanting a taste of him could open it with one swipe of powerful claws. He didn't sleep much, and when the mockingbirds and cardinals tuned up at daylight he crawled out, tired and grumpy, and rebuilt his fire. Without his morning coffee, he'd go no place fast.

An early hawk wheeled overhead, and hoot-owls were talking back and forth in the distance. But Oscar Parmelee preferred the sound of traffic and gunshots, and the pressure of town people close around him — people he understood and could dispense without thought or regret.

Leaving his tent set up and putting out the fire with great care, he set off upstream. He followed the bank as closely as the blackberry and rattan and smilax vines would allow, keeping a lookout for the cut-bank he wanted. The sun rose, and the heat trapped under the canopy of trees soon drenched him with sweat. His hat collected moisture under the band, and he had to stop frequently to wipe his face and neck with his bandana. He was still big and strong, but he'd gotten out of condition somewhere along the way. He was stopping to rest much too often.

Finally he found the place before

mid-afternoon. The big hickory overhanging the stream was unmistakable. Though the flood had washed out even more soil beneath the bank, he knew this was the spot where he had left the stash — and his two dead companions. Now he rather regretted killing them. If they still lived, they would share the blame if things went wrong.

Grunting, he climbed down the slippery bank, holding on to thick roots bared by the action of the flood, and stood in shallows where there had been deep water before. Bending, he peered into the darkness behind the tangle of roots.

Of course the bodies were gone — already found and noted and bringing their own set of problems. But surely that weighted ice chest couldn't have just floated away. The thought of messing around further in that hollow, where he was certain he could see scaly bodies gleaming where moccasins lurked, filled him with gloom — but it had to be done.

He pulled off his shirt and pants, took the flashlight from his backpack, and broke off a long, straight sapling. Where there were snakes, you needed a stick, he had learned at his daddy's knee.

The stink of mud, the coffee-colored water, and the slimy algae clinging to everything filled him with disgust. As he entered the hole, he heard a hiss and shone his light into the cottony-white maws of two moccasins, coiled on a shelf of mud at the back of the opening. Their odor was strong.

'You can stay right there,' he muttered. 'I don't intend to come anyplace close to you.'

He knelt in the water and felt around with one hand, holding the light on the snakes to make sure they didn't move any closer.

Nothing.

He tucked the light under an exposed root and used both hands to dig frantically in the muck. He even edged much closer to the moccasins than he intended to, but there was nothing there to be found.

Cursing, he backed out of the hole, wiggled between the roots, and stood again, knee-deep in the creek. There was no spot between there and the river that could hide something as big as the ice chest. If someone had taken it away and hidden it again, it would be upstream. He didn't even consider its having been swept out into the river and away to the Gulf of Mexico, so he moved on, scanning both banks with intense care.

He had seen only two very young alligators along the way. But when he came to a deep bend, where the current branch of the creek had created an island of mud overlooking a deep-looking hole of water, he stopped short. His heart lurched, and he felt bile rise in his throat.

On that mud bank lay a half dozen big gators, their lazy eyes opening as he came into sight. The biggest, a male some twelve feet long, opened his mouth and gave a grunt. Then he began to move toward the water, hissing like a teakettle.

Oscar recalled something else from his childhood. Never try to outrun an alligator on land; the creatures could catch a man over a short distance — and in the woods you can't get up much speed.

Even as that thought occurred to him, the gator crossed the waterhole with four powerful strokes of his tail and started up the slope toward him. The speed it made on those short, crooked legs was awesome. It might be more curious than hungry, but Parmelee had no intention of finding out.

He went up an overgrown persimmon tree as if he were still a boy, shinnying up eight feet to the first branches. Then he squirreled up through those to the highest point that would hold his weight. From there he stared down into the marble eyes below.

After a time, the rest of the gators joined the big bull, and they all lay down under the tree for a rest. They had done this before — and sometimes they had been rewarded for their efforts with a snack.

7

Death and Taxes

Stephen Parker wasn't satisfied with the outcome of his assignment in Nichayac County. He felt there was still work to be done there, though he had no intention of returning in person. The thought of Lena McCarver's slanted black eyes gleaming at him through the car window was enough to insure that.

He kept worrying at the problem until he came up with an idea. The IRS was always interested in people who claimed to make no money. That Choa fellow, if his claim were true, must have failed to file returns, possibly ever in his life. That lapse would interest another federal agency — one that had cleaned up many a mess in the interest of collecting money due to the government.

With a smile widening his thin lips, Parker picked up the phone and made a call. His contact on the other end had helped him out before. George could get information out of the antiquated IRS computer system faster than anybody.

'No idea of his Social Security number?' George asked, and Parker could hear the click of keys as the man began to work on his keyboard.

'His name is Choa, which is probably his last name. They call him Possum, but that can't possibly be his first name. No idea of his SSN.'

There was a hail of clicks.

'Sorry, old chum,' George said. 'I need more time. If I can check old files, maybe get in touch with somebody down there on the ground, I should be able to find what you want. Call me in two days.'

It was more like a week, though, before Parker called George again. This time it took only a moment for George to pull up the information he wanted.

'Name's Edward Choa, SSN 451-50-9922. He began filing income tax forms in 1950 when he worked in Houston. Made good money for about ten years. He was married, but his wife didn't work.

He moved back to Nichayac County in 1960. Address was a post office box in Lanford, but later he got his mail care of a Lena McCarver on a rural route out of Templeton. He filed, though he claimed he had no income, until 1987, when he filled out a form stating he didn't make enough to file any longer and stopped. One of our agents was sent to check him out, and the report said Choa made his living by fishing, trapping and trading for food. The case was closed — and nobody else ever felt it was worth following up on.'

'Dead end, then,' Parker said. 'But thanks anyway.'

'Hold on. I showed this to my supervisor, and he felt it was worth reopening. After all, *nobody* can live on nothing. We think we might have a case for going down there and investigating this old man again. He may not make much, but with interest and penalties, he'll owe a bigger sum now.'

Parker grinned. 'Good work, George. I think that Choa guy might be involved with drug-running, so maybe you can catch him on the taxes. Let me know what happens, will you?'

He hung up the phone and turned to stare out the window. By God, he was going to get that fellow yet! And, if there was any way to do it, he'd try to catch that old McCarver dame in the same sweep of the net.

★ ★ ★

Ranse Cole was angry. No sooner was he rid of the DEA bunch than here came the Internal Revenuers, a man named Rambard and his partner, bugging him about Possum Choa of all people. He told them all he knew — which wasn't much — and he could see they didn't believe him. Then the idiots had the nerve to threaten, very subtly but unmistakably, that if he didn't cooperate to suit them his *own* taxes might get audited.

Cole was so mad he could have spit tacks. With wicked intent, he sent the IRS men out to meet with Lena McCarver. If anyone deserved to get crossways with that crazy old woman, Cole chuckled to himself, Rambard and his partner were the ones.

He leaned back, breathing deeply to get his heart rate back into order, and thought about young Mike Kramer, even now busily delving into the courthouse computer system. Might the boy be able to look into federal files?

He buzzed for Myra. 'See if Mike can spare me a minute, will you?' he asked. 'I need to ask him a question or two.'

When Kramer ambled into the office, Cole greeted him warmly. 'You're doing good work, boy,' he said. 'What you found out about that fellow I asked you to check up on came in handy. I think I know who his big boss may be. You found any trace that somebody's been tapping into our system here?' he added.

As usual when talking about his specialty, Kramer flushed scarlet, making his freckles stand out. 'There's been more outsiders poking into your system than insiders,' he said. 'You need better security codes. And you need to restrict the number of people who know 'em to ones who can be trusted. There's somebody in our area who regularly snoops into the system.'

'That's just the kind of info I need,' Cole said. He folded his hands across his paunch. 'You suppose — we're just talkin' hypothetically, now — might you be able to hack into the Internal Revenue Service files?'

Kramer's face flamed even redder, and his grin widened. 'That's why I got put in jail, Sheriff. I can break into anything I darn well please, but I got caught in the IRS files. Straightened out my uncle's tax mess without him payin' a dime, but don't tell 'em that. What do you need?'

Ranse Cole felt a warm feeling rise in his chest. He'd been right in pulling this young man out of the county jail. It was a damn good thing the state prisons were too full to hold everybody. He was going to find out some things he needed to know — and Michael Kramer was going to help him do it.

'Here's what I need,' he said, pushing his notes across the desk.

★　★　★

August Rambard was sweating, even though it was late September. The air conditioner had gone out on the trip from Austin, and the inside of the Pontiac could have baked bread. The map on his lap was limp as he refolded it to follow the thin line that was the road. The oil-top was better than dirt, but still was full of potholes where logging trucks had turned off into tracks into the woods. The county map was large-scale, so it was fairly easy to check off the homes they passed, dirt tracks that seemed to wander away to no place in particular, and the long lanes that often led to abandoned houses or barns.

When they came to the turnoff that marked the McCarver house, he realized that anywhere they went from here would be heading *out*. Why would an old woman want to live by herself way down here?

His assistant, Curley, turned into the lane and bumped over a badly kept cattle-guard. Just beyond, there was a wide stretch of pasture that ended in a wall of trees so thick he couldn't imagine how they'd missed the attention of the loggers.

As the car jounced along, there came the shrill cry of a hawk and the raucous cawing of crows. A fox skittered across the dusty lane ahead of the car, and Curley slowed even more. Breaking down here would be a bother, because there was no telephone service within miles of this area — and their cell phones were far out of range of any carrier.

They rounded a sharp bend and saw the warped gray wood of a gate. Curley pulled up and they both stared at the house beyond the falling-down fence and the overgrown yard. On the porch, an old-fashioned swing moved uneasily in a gust of breeze, while a scarred tomcat stared them down from his perch on the top step.

August opened the door and stepped out into the talc-like dust. 'Anybody home?' he called. 'Miz McCarver, are you here?'

There was no response from the house, though the cat thrust one hind leg into the air and proceeded to wash his bottom industriously.

'She's not here,' he said over his shoulder to Curley, who was locking the car. 'Might as well look around — see if she's got more than she ought, on an income of three thousand dollars a year.'

He was beginning to feel that this would be a washout. Nobody who could afford it would live here on purpose. He wished now he had opened the rickety mailbox at the main road to see what kind of mail she received.

He creaked open the gate and motioned Curley to go ahead to the house, while he looked around for anything suspicious in the outbuildings. But the sagging shed contained only a dusty old Chevy, cobwebs, and rotted bushel baskets. The only other structure was quite obviously a privy. He stuck his head inside, but a wasp zoomed at his head, and he ducked back and shut the door.

He moved toward the back porch. The door was nailed shut, so he went around the side of the house to the front where

Curley was standing, back hunched, staring into the gloom of the interior.

'I don't like this much, Augie,' Curley said. 'I feel like something's watching us. Besides, the floor's so soft we might fall through.'

'I'll go inside,' Rambard said. 'You see if there's anything hid in that wood-box on the end of the porch.'

He took a tentative step inside and closed the screen door behind him. He found himself in a room that extended the entire depth of the house, combining the functions of sitting room and kitchen. There were two doors on his right, one leading into what was obviously a bedroom, the other into the half of the house that was about to fall down. She used a wood-burning cook stove, he saw, noting that this indicated poverty of a pretty dire sort. That and the privy. Still, he wouldn't give up just yet. She might know something about Choa and his activities.

There wasn't much food in the pantry — home-canned stuff in glass jars, a sack of flour in a bin, a tin canister filled with

143

cornmeal, some herbs hanging from hooks in the back wall. She didn't eat well, that was certain.

He moved into the bedroom to look under the mattress. Women always hid stuff there. On the small table by the window sat a kerosene lamp and a big, thick book. Maybe a family bible. Looked antique. He reached a tentative finger to open it, finding it filled with crabbed handwriting whose ink had faded to palest brown. He bent to squint at the letters, then stiffened.

'It isn't polite to poke around in a lady's belongin's,' said a sharp voice behind him.

Rambard felt his heart leap. Light steps tapped toward him around the table, and a tiny shape came into his field of vision.

'Another gover'ment man, I take it?' She stared up into his face, her black eyes sparking with fury. 'Nobody else would be rude or foolish enough to meddle with my property. You come out here with the young idiot on the porch, and we'll sort this out.'

Suddenly Rambard was standing straight

again, but he was unable to control his body. She marched him out to stand beside Curley, who was frozen, a look of horror on his face, over the kindling box where a copperhead snake twined and wriggled among sticks of wood. The younger man's hand was within striking range, but the snake ignored it. The woman smiled, a quirk of the lip that was more forbidding than a snarl, and snapped her fingers. Curley straightened and Rambard felt his own paralysis ease.

'You can't . . . ' he began, but again his jaw froze in place.

'I *can*,' said Lena McCarver. 'It's *you* who can't. You go back wherever you came from and erase my name off your books. I never make enough to pay any taxes, anyway. Tell anybody else that wants to come snooping that they'd best forget I exist at all. You hear me?'

Rambard managed the faintest hint of a nod, and he meant it. No wonder that other agent had marked this off the books. There was no money here, that was certain. And this wasn't the kind of situation you could put in a report — not without getting sent up for psychiatric evaluation.

'There's been too many idiots coming to my house to suit me,' she was saying. 'And I'll have no more truck with the outside, if I can help it. When the postman brings my stuff every month I'll let him come in, but anybody else better have a pretty good reason — or they may find themselves dodging water moccasins in the creek or bobcats in the woods.'

Rambard nodded. She meant it. Who had opened up this can of worms? DEA Agent Parker was the one — and if he ever had a chance, August Rambard intended to audit Stephen Parker within an inch of his life.

★   ★   ★

Although there had always been odd things going on in and around the swamp country, those tended to be what the river-bottom people considered normal. Killings were fairly common, but everyone knew the reason for them — and could have put a finger on the killer, if

146

they had been willing.

Drug dealing had gone on as well, though the resistance of the regular population had held it down to a minimum. This present drug deal, however, had been like a stick driven into an anthill, stirring up more activity than anyone had seen before.

As Lena went about hiding the turnoff to her road, she was also considering this nasty business and the effect it was having on her and her friends and neighbors. Almost absent-mindedly, she whisked dead brush across the outer edge of the cattle-guard, pulled the sagging metal gate closed, and searched for the rusty chain and the stiff lock that she so seldom used.

When all was secure, she realized that she must get word to Irene. Boze Blair had a key to that lock, but he needed to know to bring it with him when he returned with her groceries. Irene could call him, and then they would both know.

With a sigh, she unlocked the gate again and trudged back to her house to get her car out of the shed. She drove cautiously out of her lane and found the blacktop that would, after a while, bring her to Irene Follette's farm.

She realized she had seen more people in the past two months than she usually came face to face with in two years. That was not a particularly good or useful thing, and she hoped it wouldn't continue. She was quite happy alone, with the very rare visits from her regulars to keep her somewhat attached to the outside world.

Turning at last into the Follette drive, she braked in front of the wide front porch. Irene's dog Wolf roused, wandered out from under the yaupon bushes that fringed the veranda, and sniffed her tires thoroughly.

''Lo, Wolf,' Lena said as she got her stiff legs out of the vehicle and stood. 'Yoo-hoo! Irene!' she called.

Echoes bounced back from the heavy woods that curved around the sides and back of the place. For a moment there was silence. Then Lena heard a faint call from behind the house.

'Did she call for help?' she asked Wolf,

who looked puzzled and dashed away toward the sheds at the back.

Lena followed as quickly as her legs allowed, and when she arrived she could see Wolf staring beneath the sagging shed roof. As she approached, the dog went in, and she could hear his inquiring whine, for the wolf-dog didn't bark.

The strong September sunshine lit the place fairly well — enough to show Lena the shape of the artist, who lay across the grain bin, her back twisted painfully.

'Lordy, Irene, what's happened to you?' Lena asked, but she was already easing her shoulder under the body of the much taller woman. Irene gave a muffled shriek.

'It's all right,' she said. 'I've got to get off here. You go ahead and see if you can get me straightened out on the ground, if you can.'

Lena struggled to accomplish that, and at last Irene lay straight — or at least straighter — beside the bin, though her back still seemed to be out of place.

'I got my car out front,' Lena panted. 'If we can get you in, I'll get you far enough up the road for one of the neighbors to drive you to town.'

Irene turned her head, her pale eyes wide.

'No. I don't want anyone to know where I am. Somebody came out here early this morning while I was feeding the chickens and Wolf was on his morning run, and tried to make me tell him where those drugs are. He knocked me over the bin, and my back went out. Then he laughed and went off and left me.' Irene paused to gain her breath. 'Take me to *your* house, Lena. I'll be safe there while I get better. You know all kinds of healing methods, and if you can't help me I'll just stay tied in a knot. Better that than dead, which is what that stranger threatened — if I didn't tell him what he wanted to know.'

The older woman snorted with disgust. 'That his track?' she asked, pointing to a print of a western boot outlined in the dust of the floor. When Irene nodded, she spat carefully into the center of the footprint and said something very unflattering about its owner. 'You think you might be able to walk a little, if I get the car up close?' she asked.

Irene got her elbows down and pushed upward. She nodded, gritting her teeth. 'You get the car. I'll make it.'

Lena turned and asked, 'You need anything from the house? Clothes, your purse? I'll lock it up when I come out.'

It took some doing, but at last Lena had her passenger in the old Chevy, with Wolf running desperately behind, headed back to her own country. Only then did she think about Boze Blair and his key.

'Damn! I should have called Boze before we locked up your house and left. I'm going to lock up my gate, and he needs to get in with my supplies.'

'Mail him a note,' Irene said. 'I have stamps and envelopes in my purse.'

They arrived at Lena's gate before mid-afternoon, and there Lena wrote a note to Boze on a page from Irene's notebook. Once the stamped envelope was in the rusted mailbox, she drove through the gate and locked it behind her.

As the Chevy crept over the bumps and ruts of her lane, Lena was thinking hard. With so many town people coming down here trying to find things, it was time to take a stand. Nobody had a right to abuse her neighbors.

'You got any idea who that was who beat you up?' she asked Irene, who was stretched uneasily along the back seat, grunting when they hit a particularly deep rut.

Lena watched her in the mirror behind the sun flap as she opened her eyes and looked thoughtful. 'You know, I think I do know him,' Irene said. 'Name's Fielding, I think. He works for Nathaniel Farmer sometimes, though I think he has other and less legal sources of income.'

'Harland Fielding?' asked Lena, who had good reason to recognize that name. 'That's the feller who was so bound and determined to get my timber. He came and he came, nearly driving me out of my wits.' She slowed the car and peered back into the dust, whistling for the dog. 'You about had enough, boy?' she asked. 'You can get in the car, but stay off the seat.' The dog came panting up and climbed into the back of the Chevy beside his mistress.

Lena was thinking. Possum Choa needed to know that Irene had been attacked. King, too, would be interested . . . and angry. It was time for the swamp people to pull together.

It was a struggle to get Irene into the yard and up the steps to the porch. While she drooped on the swing, Lena dashed inside and made up her own bed fresh. For the time being she'd sleep on a pallet on the floor.

After supper, Lena stretched herself on the thick pad of quilts and stared up at the kitchen ceiling, with its fancy pattern of leak-rings darkening the ancient paper. Tomorrow she'd need to raise the signals that meant for the swamp-people to gather at her house for a pow-wow.

She closed her eyes, and Lone, alert to her moods, crept up close to her ankles and began to purr.

★   ★   ★

She drifted off to sleep and found herself across the forest, down toward the maze of streams that laced the edge of the

153

swamp. There was King's place. But having no idea where to look for Possum's cabin, she let herself go free on the wind.

She found him at last, camped beside a creek some two miles from the river, and wondered what had taken him there. She would raise her signal tomorrow, and one of the old men would surely see it, in time . . .

Then she felt something else below her. Something alien, shallow and dark.

Who was down there on that creek? What was he doing . . . in a tree? Intrigued, she let her awareness sink to treetop level and found herself staring with unseen eyes at the man who was crouched there. Below him, their scaly backs gleaming softly in sprinkles of moonlight, a half-dozen alligators dozed. From time to time, one would trundle off to the creek and a late-evening snack, but at any time there were at least three standing watch. Soon, she knew, they would grow weary of their vigil, and their captive would be able to escape. And that, it seemed to her, might be a great pity.

Could she, in her dream state, communicate with Possum Choa? It was worth trying. She rose into the night breeze and sped back to the spot where she had seen him. There, she eddied over his sleeping body, wondering how to insert her dream into his dream.

'Choa! Choa! Look along Sandbar Creek! Among the gators!' That was the message she struggled to convey. Then, exhausted, she whipped back along the trail of her selfhood and regained the sanctuary of her aching body.

★　★　★

Lena opened her eyes and stared into darkness. She could hear the breathing of her guest in the bedroom, the light thud of Lone's tough old heart, the creaking of aged boards, and the whisper of shrubbery outside her warped windows. Nothing troubled the land around her home.

Had she reached Choa's sleeping mind? she wondered. But she could only wait and see.

8

Setting Up a Messenger

Choa woke in the middle of the night with a feeling that there was something he needed to do. He tried to think of what it might be, but nothing came to mind. He'd settled the drug question for good and all, he knew. Nothing ever came out of that sinkhole.

The boy Wim was safely back home — Choa had followed secretly to make certain of it. Wim was tough and smart, but there were things going on in the bottomlands that might be dangerous for a child, so Choa made sure, without giving the boy any sign that he was behind him.

What else could there be? Still, something brought him up from his pallet of dead leaves and set him moving, well before the star patterns reached their midnight position. He'd learned long ago to follow his hunches, for they were too often important and accurate. He even knew which direction to take — he was heading for the creek where he had first hidden the ice chest. His legs, still strong for all his sixty years, covered the ground at a rapid rate, cutting across loops of meandering streams and using deer trails. By midnight he found himself following the narrow branches that were the upper reaches of the stream above the gator hole.

When he came to the wider part, where the big bend and the eddy had hidden the chest for a while, he realized that only one alligator was resting on the low bank. Two more lurked at the edge of the water. He looked around carefully.

Slipping along with all the skill he had learned from his father and grandfather, Choa scouted out the area along the creek bank. Crouching low, he checked the treetops; lying flat along the ground, he surveyed the surface of the forest floor.

He spotted the man in the huge persimmon tree, just as he had found

Wim up a tree earlier. Once he knew where the man was, he also knew where the rest of the alligators were.

Easing backward, he came to the higher edge of the creek and checked about for something heavy. A pine knot came beneath his groping fingers, and he grabbed it with satisfaction. Pulling it free of the clinging dirt and threadlike roots of vines, he hefted it, found a clear area through which to fling it, and pitched it into the deeper water.

It hit with a solid splash, the sort a leaping fish might make if it rose for a late-night meal. Choa heard a rustling, grunting, slithering noise as the gators around the persimmon tree roused and turned toward the sound of potential food. He watched as the creatures returned to their regular habitat.

When the last had passed, he moved toward the tree. His arrival was a shock, it was clear, to the man who was just dropping to the ground.

Then everything became clear to Choa. In the confetti of moonlight drifting through the overarching branches, he saw and recognized the face of the man in the boat.

'Well, Mr. Parmelee,' he said, 'I've been waiting for you. Seems as if you left something down here in my country that you want mighty bad.'

Parmelee turned toward him, his scratched face pale and filled with hope. 'You found it?' Parmelee sank to the ground as if his knees had given way. 'What'd you do with it? I'll pay big money to get it back.'

'Oh, I wouldn't take any money for it, even if I still had the stuff,' Choa said. 'But I can show you where it went.'

'How far is it?' Parmelee asked. 'I been in that tree half the day and most of the night. I'm about wore out with perchin' on that skinny limb.' Then he looked up, alarmed. 'What did you mean, if you still had it?'

'You'll see,' Choa said. 'You want to go now, or you want to rest a while? It'll be easier in the daylight.'

Parmelee looked warily toward the creek. 'I'd just as soon move away from here, over into the woods. Then I could use some rest, flat on my back with no gators starin' up at me.'

Possum Choa grinned. Finding this killer helpless in the woods was better luck than he'd ever dreamed of having.

* * *

Choa roused Parmelee as soon as there was enough light to walk by. Scratched, bruised, and hungry, the drug dealer grumbled a bit before he got himself together enough to travel.

Choa had tickled a couple of big perch out of their morning doze. Skewered on sweetgum rods and crisped quickly over a small fire, they provided enough breakfast to keep his captive going.

He intended to show Oscar Parmelee exactly where his precious stuff was hidden. Then he'd let him go out and tell whoever he wanted to about it. Parmelee would be hard-put to find the sinkhole again on his own. And even if he did, there was no way to plumb its depths without draining several thousand square acres of swamp and bottomland. And if the pusher returned with some of those for whom he worked, well, that would be all right, too. People sometimes came into the swamp — and never went out again.

The two men wandered for miles, it seemed, around deer paths, spring branches, creek meanderings and the loops of the river. By the time they came over the ridge above the sinkhole, Parmelee was staggering with exhaustion, but he was hanging on in the hope he was about to recover his stash. Choa wanted to laugh, but he suppressed the urge as he led his flagging companion down a slight slope to the tangle of briers near the edge of the morass.

As Parmelee stumbled to a halt beside him, Choa pointed into the middle of the thick gray-green mess before them. 'I put it in there, in the hole behind the briers. Nothin' has ever come out of that bog in all the years my folks have lived here. Every twenty or thirty years it turns — something about the swamp gas does that, I think — and the bones of deer and cows and men and petrified logs and all sorts of things roll up and over and down again. Maybe in a couple of decades you might come back and camp out here to wait. But that ice chest is *gone*, as far as the here and now goes.'

Parmelee dropped to his knees, staring in despair at the gluey mess. 'It wasn't *just* the drugs,' he whimpered. 'That would be bad enough. But they smuggled in somethin' really valuable — more than the million or so the pure cocaine would bring — that the Big Boss wanted mighty bad. Diamonds, it might be. Or maybe parts or plans for a nuclear bomb. And now it's all lost!'

He turned to Choa as he rose, and there was murder in his red-rimmed eyes. But the Indian had slid away silently and swiftly, and now he watched from a clump of saw vines as Parmelee blundered about the edge of the hole, probing with a dead branch he had scavenged.

Nodding quietly, Choa decided that it might be a good thing to let Parmelee find his own way out of the swamp. He had no intention of doing anything specific or personal to those who might return with Parmelee, but he also had a deep sense of the realities of this country.

The swamp was truly unforgiving. A bunch of townies who couldn't find their way out of their own back yards could easily wander around in circles until they lay down and died of pure discouragement. Which, once he thought about it, was a pretty fair and just way for them to go.

So when Parmelee began his attempt to get back to roads and people and all the things he understood and could deal with, Choa was there, leaving traces that even a blind idiot could follow. Only when he gained the unmistakable paths along the big creek that ended at the river did Choa give up his surveillance and turn his weary steps toward home and his own familiar pallet bed.

It would take Parmelee a long time to bumble his way to the nearest pull-out where a dirt road ended at the river, even if he turned right instead of left at the bigger stream. It would take even longer for him to convince those he worked for that he was telling the truth. And even if he was able to do that, he still might be held responsible and killed for the loss of whatever treasure accompanied the drugs in that ice chest.

The thought didn't bother Choa a bit.

If someone came back to search, Choa would know. It wasn't only old Lena who had watchers in the woods.

★   ★   ★

It had tickled the life out of Sheriff Cole when August Rambard and his sidekick came skittering back into Templeton, tight-lipped and unwilling to talk about their visit to Lena McCarver. They assured him that they had all the information they needed and left without even stopping to eat lunch.

He'd been chuckling over that for a couple of days when the cell phone rang. He cursed softly as he picked the thing up, and just as he feared, it was Harland Fielding.

'We've got a problem,' the man began, without even the pretense of courtesy. 'One of our people — ' Cole had a shrewd idea he meant Oscar Parmelee.

164

' — has located our 'property' down in the swamps. We'll need help getting it out — sounds as if it's sunk in a bog down there.'

Ransome Cole suddenly knew that if he went along with this assumption that he was in the pockets of Fielding and his boss, he would never be his own man again. Even if it meant danger for himself or his wife, he had to make a stand now.

'Harland,' he said in his most peaceable tone, 'I don't give a damn whether you ever find those drugs or not. And if it's Parmelee who told you about 'em, you better either turn him in or get him out of my county before my deputy can get over there. You hear me?'

A second of stunned silence followed his words, and he felt a surge of pride fill his overweight body. Whatever happened, he'd taken his life out of their dirty hands. If it came down to it, he'd shoot Harland Fielding down without a second thought and know he'd done a good thing for everybody he served.

There was a click as Fielding hung up. Ranse called his office. When Myra answered, he said, 'You get Philips over where Harland Fielding stays. Tell him to watch his step and take Steve Goddard with him in another car. Call Wash Shipp and fill him in — he might want to help. I'm going to be out of town tonight; keep this under wraps unless somebody really needs to know.'

Next he called his sister-in-law, Ellen Gooding, down at Noonan, seventy miles south. 'El? I need to get Mae out of town for a while,' he said. 'Can you come up and get her, or should I bring her down myself?'

'What're you up to, Ranse?' came the quick reply.

'I've turned over a new leaf, El,' he replied. 'I'm goin' after some of the big baddies here in Templeton, and I don't want Mae in the line of fire. I just told off Harland — you 'member Harland Fielding?'

He heard her quick gasp of comprehension. 'I'll come get her, Ranse. Be there before dark, if you can put me up for the night.'

He thought for a moment. 'I'll meet

you halfway at Lewton. I don't want either one of you to spend tonight in the house. I intend to . . . go somewhere else, myself.'

He almost let his plan out, but just in time it occurred to him that if his computer system in the jail and courthouse could be tapped, they could tap his private phone, too. He didn't quite know how the technology worked, but the possibility of leaking his plan too soon was something to avoid.

'Is it that bad?' El asked.

'I can't say for certain, but I've known that man for more than forty years, and I don't intend to take a chance on him. He's mean clear through to the bone, and you know it as well as I do. I'll meet you at Cal's in Lewton at about five-thirty,' he added, 'if you can make it by then.'

'I'll be waiting for you, Ranse. You know how much I care about my sister. If you're that worried about her, I'm worried twice as much. You just get there. I'll be waiting in my car.'

With a sigh of relief, Cole turned toward the courthouse and his parking space. He'd leave his official car in the county lot. There was no way he wanted to take off in something as easily identified as the marked police car. His old Ford looked like about a thousand other cars in town, and for the first time he appreciated that. Sticking out like a sore thumb was a good way to get your head blown off.

He returned to Templeton from Lewton about eight-thirty that evening and turned into the next street over from his house. He'd had the folks at Cal's pack him some sandwiches and fill his coffee thermos. He kept a blanket and sleeping bag in the Ford, but if he lay down he'd go to sleep, and tonight he needed to stay wide awake.

He crept through the shrubbery between property lines and crossed the back yard that abutted his own, then tiptoed to the chain-link fence between the properties and peered out through the thick foliage.

The light he'd left on inside lit the bushes outside the window, and its glow, filtering down the hallway, shone softly through the glass of the back door. He'd planned to have as much light as made sense, both in order to seem natural and to see anybody who might be lurking around the place. He'd left the front porch light on, too.

So far, he seemed to be the only one lurking. He drifted around to his neighbor Mack Reynolds' side yard, where a thick bunch of japonica made good cover. He lay flat and crawled into the bushes, pleased that he could still move so silently.

From that position, he could see the front door, well lit. The side door was directly opposite him, lit by the street lamp at the end of the Reynolds drive, and he could also see the back door, where the glow of the lamp would make anyone approaching it quite visible.

He might spend a miserable night watching a house where nothing was going to happen, but he knew he could never have gone in and slept easily after hearing the venomous note in Fielding's voice and the silence after he made his stand. There were unsolved killings in his county that he was morally certain could be laid at that man's door. Friends or enemies were all one to that snake! Thank God he'd never taken money from Fielding. The favors he had done had been petty, and for that he was grateful.

He settled down, waiting with the patience of an old deer hunter, while the night ticked away on his watch. From time to time a car passed, and most of those he recognized. First came Sam Dutton, going to his job on the swing shift at the foundry. Then it was Elizabeth Stafford, coming home from her seven-to-three shift at the hospital.

It was the car he didn't recognize that roused him to full alertness. It was a nondescript gray Chevy with patches of rust on its fenders. Its engine, however, was quiet — which made him suspicious. It paused beside the curb thirty yards up the street. Then it came on, and he could just see someone walking along beside it, stooped so he wouldn't be seen by anyone glancing out a window. Once level with Cole's front door, the vehicle stopped, and the walker raced up and flung something against the door; it hit with a loud thump.

He was fast, but Cole had made it a habit to note appearances, and he thought he could ID the man if he saw him again. Tall and skinny, he ran as if he had something wrong with his right leg. His hair flashed pale under the street lamp — blond or maybe going gray. He had the longest arms Ranse had ever seen on anybody.

Then he was back in the car and it was racing down the street, the men inside now unworried by any noise it might make.

Ranse laid his face on his folded arms and waited. In about the time it would have taken him to reach the front door from his bedroom, there came a blast of noise. Even with his face covered he could see a blinding flash of light. Then he shot out of the japonicas and pounded on Mack Reynolds' back door. 'Mack! Call the fire department! Call the police! They just bombed my house!' he shouted, before jumping over the low hedge into his own yard.

The garden hose was connected, as always in the fall, to keep Mae's chrysanthemums watered. He turned it on full and hauled its length into the window of Mae's sewing room, which was already filling with smoke. He dragged the hose further, keeping its stream directed at the open door into the living room.

The front wall was a mass of flames, which were coming around the door facing, and the rug was giving off a horrible smell and volumes of thick black smoke. He could hear the crackle of fire overhead, too, and knew the roof was burning. But he couldn't be two places at once, and he kept drenching everything in sight so the fire wouldn't get fully involved inside the house.

By the time sirens told him the fire department was there, he had the interior fire quenched. The harsh sizzle of the fire-hose's stream on the roof and front wall brought him out at last to stand beside Oliver Stitch, the fire chief and his long-time drinking buddy.

Ollie looked at him intently between

barked orders to firemen, who were getting the last of the burning shrubbery under control and chopping a hole in the roof to make sure there was no fire in the attic. 'This was no accident, Ranse,' he said. 'What happened?'

Cole sighed. 'I crossed Fielding today, big time. And his boss, and his boss's boss, if any. Took a stand, Ollie, for the first time since I can remember. Cost me a bundle — did you really have to cut up my roof?'

Stitch didn't laugh, though it was intended as a joke. 'I figured something like that as soon as I saw your front porch. That was a bomb, if I ever saw one. They didn't waste any time. How'd you get Mae out? Is she all right?'

Cole nodded. 'I got her out of town. I expected somethin' like this, though maybe not so bold. I've got an idea old Harland's brought in some outside muscle, because bombing's not the normal way down here. Burn down a man's house, maybe, but not by bombing it. Shoot his cattle or beat him up or even kill him, but not quite this way. This's

173

somethin' new in this county.'

Wash Shipp came over, shaking his head. As police chief, he had seen most of the mischief in town for the past thirteen years, but Cole could see by his expression that this had really gotten to him. The two weren't friends — they'd been on opposite sides of just about every political issue for decades — but they weren't exactly enemies, either. The big black officer was one of those straight-arrow people that Cole was now wishing he'd been himself.

Now he reached for Cole's hand. 'Man, I'm really sorry about this. I heard what you said to Ollie, and it makes me boil. We both know that Nate Farmer's behind Harland Fielding, but I haven't a clue as to who's behind Nate. You have any notion?'

'I didn't even know for sure it was Nate Farmer,' Ranse admitted. 'All I knew was what I called in to my office yesterday after I heard from Fielding. Did you find Parmelee at the Holiday Inn?'

Wash shook his head. 'They'd flown the coop, soon as you told Fielding to take a hike, I'd guess. But we'll get 'em now that we've got something real and solid we can set our teeth into. Sooner or later we'll hook Fielding up with that car — you got the number? — and hang him on a charge of terrorist activity. That covers a lot of stuff, enough to hold him while we get more on him.'

But Cole was staring at his ruined porch and scorched and blasted wall and door. Mae was going to pitch a fit — then he realized that the insurance would cover this. They could fix up the place real well. Then maybe they'd sell it and move down close to her sister. It was time he thought about retiring, anyway. If the Old Guard biggies who ran things here were going to bring in really nasty folks to do their dirty work around Templeton, he didn't much care to be involved in trying to catch them. There was nothing like a real shock to bring you to your senses, he realized.

He turned to Shipp and gave him the license number and a detailed description of the bomber, but already he was thinking about the good fishing spots he'd noted down over the years. Retirement while he was still fit might be a very satisfactory idea, and with his pension he'd be in good enough shape to last a long time.

No sir, he'd let younger and braver people figure out this mess. He and Mae were going to live a little bit, in the time they had left.

9

Pow-wow

When King Deport made his weekly tour of his domain, he always checked the signal atop the big tree at Lena McCarver's place. He could see it from only one clearing that gave him a glimpse of the treetop, and he always made sure no flag flew, warning that the old woman needed something. In forty years, only twice had he seen the thing, and both times it had signaled a real problem for the people living along the river.

Now that the leaves were beginning to yellow and shrivel, it was easier to spot that distant speck. It had been years since King could check the flag with unaided eyes, so he always kept his old binoculars around his neck. Now he raised them and stared toward the tree. Something yellow snapped in the morning breeze.

Uh-oh! Lena had two flags up,

separated by a small spot of red. That meant everybody needed to come. Because of the contour of the land, the blast of her shotgun didn't reach his place — he refused to consider that he might be getting deaf — but he would have bet that Choa was already on his way.

'Drat!' he muttered. 'I need to set a fresh batch of trotlines. Still, I better get goin'.'

He trudged off toward the river, for it was easier to follow it to Lena's property line and cut across her woods to the house. Going through the thick tangles of briers and brush, stretches of swamp, and network of creeks was more than his old bones were willing to tackle these days.

When he came along the woods-path leading to the old gray house, he was surprised to see Lena's Chevy sitting before her gate. Seldom did the old woman drive the car, though somehow she kept it running.

When he tapped on the porch post, he was even more surprised to look past her approaching figure to see someone coming out of the bedroom door. 'Miz Follette?' Now why would she be here, and without her own car?

Lena gestured for him to sit in the wicker chair while she and Irene occupied the swing. 'You catch your breath, Mister Deport. We got a bit of time till Choa gets here. Then we got to figure out what to do about the folks who've been messing around down here and bothering us. Irene got roughed up this morning, and it's time to call a halt to such doings.'

King stared at the younger woman, feeling the heat rise in his neck and face. 'You mean somebody actually laid *hands* on you?' he asked.

'Harland Fielding caught me in my shed, getting the feed for my chickens. He shook me and hit me and knocked me over the grain bin. Put my back out, but Lena's got me pretty well put together again,' the tall woman replied.

'Sim Fielding's boy? *That* Harland?' King asked, unable to believe that someone he had known as a child could possibly abuse a woman. 'You sure?'

'I'm sure. And he threatened to go

179

clear to the river, beating up people until he found someone who would tell him where to find that box of stuff. Kimball Fitts disappears as soon as a car bumps along the road. But Mrs. Dooley has a bunch of kids and never gets far from her house. So she might be in trouble. I've heard about drug busts and such,' Irene continued. 'But never before did I see the dealers raise such a stink about losing their shipment,'

'Never you worry about the Dooleys,' said Lena. 'That young Wim will take care of anybody who bothers his mama. You can bank on it.'

King sighed. 'What bothers me is thinking about what it might be that makes this particular drug shipment so valuable. Why should the bosses bother about it? They've been losing shipments to lawmen for years without so much fuss.'

'Think about it!' Lena interrupted. 'What *else* is in that box, along with the cocaine or heroin, that makes it so valuable? Oscar Parmelee never was caught before that I ever heard about, though the narcs knew about him. The shipper must have thought his whatsit was safe to send through with him.' She cocked her head inquiringly. 'You think diamonds or such?'

Irene shook her head. 'Those are little and easy to slip past inspections, according to what I've read. No, this is something that can fit into an ice chest but isn't little enough to hide in the lining of a coat.'

Their speculations were interrupted by the arrival of Choa, who appeared like a shadow from the privet bushes beyond the house and came on silent feet toward the three on the porch. 'Heard the shotgun,' he told Lena. 'Came right away.'

Lena nodded to Irene. 'Tell him,' she said, leaning back in the swing.

Once the tale was told, they sat quietly, thinking. Choa, who no longer kept up very closely with matters outside his swamp country, looked both angry and uneasy. 'We've got nasty people coming into our country. Bad things are happenin' to folks. I just yesterday showed that Parmelee fellow where I threw away that ice chest.' King grunted a protest, but Choa raised a hand for patience. 'I sent it down the big sinkhole. God himself couldn't get it out, 'less he dried up this whole country for a couple of years, and maybe not even then. I showed it to him, and then I melted out of sight and watched him stumble off, trying to find his way out. Left him some sign, just enough to keep him going right. Come to me that if I left a good trail he might bring his big boss or maybe more than one down there to work on gettin' their stuff back.'

Lena raised her head, her black eyes bright and sharp. Irene gave a deep sigh and nodded slowly, and King felt a wide grin spreading across his own face. 'You get those bastards down here where they don't know their tails from a hole in the ground, they're going to be pretty well helpless,' he said. 'They can bring guns, they can bring tools, but I'd bet my boot buttons they won't bring a lot of help. They can't afford to have the lowlifes that work for them know where that chest is. They might try to get one of their bought-and-paid-for lawmen to help, but maybe not even that.' He felt a deep chuckle rising in his chest. The thought of putting those slick townies down there beside the sinkhole tickled his fancy.

The others began to grin. King leaned back and sighed deeply. 'We can provide a lot more trouble than any of them can handle, I suspect. Just letting the country itself take care of them might be enough. I wouldn't trust most townies to keep their heads above water.'

The tomcat, draped over the edge of a step, raised one ear and sat up, looking toward the woods-road. Irene's wolf-dog came out from under the porch and bristled as he stalked toward the rickety gate.

'Somebody's coming,' King said, glancing at Lena. 'You think maybe we ought to disappear for a bit, while you deal with whoever it is?'

She looked thoughtful, her head cocked to follow the jouncing and bumping of the vehicle over the ruts and roots of the track. 'Irene and Choa might go inside. Four's too many to find here at one time.

But there's no reason in the world why my old neighbor mightn't be visiting me. You stay put, Mr. Deport. I think you and I and Lone and Wolf can handle anybody that comes poking around, even if he has had to cut my chain at the gate to get in.'

The others moved into the house and went so far as to go into the unused portion, which could give them a view of the porch without allowing them to be seen. King pulled out his pipe and stoked it with dried mullein leaves.

When he lit it, Lena nodded approvingly. 'Good for the chest and lungs,' she said. 'You're a wise man, Mr. Deport, not to clog up your innards with poison.'

She perched on the step beside the alert tomcat, scratching him behind the ears as they waited to see who was coming.

King could see dust, carried ahead of the vehicle on the brisk north breeze, before the car came into view.

Irene said, from her place of concealment, 'That's Fielding's car. I've seen him driving it in town.'

King shifted his weight and rose to lean

casually against the nearest porch post. His gnarled walnut walking stick was at hand, and he was ready for anything this whippersnapper might try to hand out.

The Cadillac pulled up amid a last swirl of dust. When the door opened, Fielding unfolded his lanky length and strode toward the gate.

'Miz McCarver?' he asked, his tone not one guaranteed to gain him any cooperation.

King didn't like people who hid their eyes behind dark glasses, which usually told him they had other things to hide. This duded-up fellow in his tan suit and shined-up cowboy boots was the kind the old man particularly didn't appreciate. He moved forward to stand behind Lena.

The old woman rose to her feet, the tomcat bristling at her side. 'What you want, sonny?' she asked in her most shriveling manner. 'You lost?'

The man pushed back his straw hat and stared at her, his lips curling. 'You don't want to get across me, old woman,' he said. 'I want some answers, and I want 'em now. One of my men came out of the swamp yesterday evening and said that scoundrel Choa put my ... goods ... into quicksand. I want to know where he lives.'

Lena sighed. 'Seems like every idiot born this century has come down here and asked me that same question. Listen hard, sonny. Nobody but Choa and God knows where he lives, and neither one has talked to me about it. It's kind of south of here is all I can tell you. And unless you had the U.S. army helping you, you'd never be able to comb out this country close enough to find his place. Now you get back into that car and hightail it out of here. I like my privacy, and there's been precious little of it to be had this summer. Federal agents! Deputies! And now drug pushers cutting my chain! I'm about out of patience with the whole kit and bilin' of you.'

She stepped off the porch, her skirt caught up in a vicious pinch in her left hand. 'Scat!' she hissed between her teeth. Lone, beside her, raised a lip and showed his incisors, while Wolf grinned his particularly wolfish grin.

Fielding took an involuntary step backward. 'Now see here,' he began, but King was now on the ground, his stick held ready to poke him in the belly.

The man stared at the strange group, his mouth working as if he longed to curse them but didn't quite dare to begin. Then he backed away, with Wolf keeping his teeth in easy reach of his knee, to the gate. There he pulled the thing shut between him and the dog.

'You don't cross me! You don't cross the man I work for! Old folks, way out in the woods this way, can have all kinds of things happen to them. Fires, hunters shooting in the woods, drugged-out kids — there's just no telling what might happen to you.'

His face was twisted with anger as he stepped into his fancy car and slammed the door. As he surged backward, twisted into a sharp turn, and zoomed recklessly out of sight, King sat down again, his stick across his lap.

'You just wait a minute,' he said to Lena. 'We'll have to go pry him out of his car, because I believe he's goin' to hit a tree along about . . . now!'

At that moment, there was a crash. The big hickory at the sharp bend, King thought, had claimed another victim.

'Come on, Choa,' he said over his shoulder. 'Let's go get the bastard out of there and send him on his way. You care if we use your car?' he asked Lena.

She nodded and went after her keys; without much conversation the four piled into her Chevy and went through the still-settling dust to the spot where the Caddy was well and truly hung up in the thicket surrounding that huge hickory.

Fielding was sprawled over the dash, his forehead sporting a lump that was already turning blue. He was out cold, though not badly hurt, Lena decided.

'Let's deliver him to his boss,' said King as they heaved him out. 'Give Farmer a shaking-up, that will.'

Possum Choa nodded. 'Maybe bring him out of his safe place, you think? Maybe bring him down here, where he's got no people around him?'

Lena smiled. 'Now wouldn't that be a useful thing?' she asked. 'If he'd come right down here where we could look him in the eye — but I don't think that could ever happen. He's not one to risk his own hide, not Nathan Farmer.'

Irene watched as they manhandled the limp shape into Lena's car. 'If you let me off at home, where I can pick up my own car, I might be able to gig him on a bit. I've known Washington Shipp since we were in college together. He might know some way to stir up the ant-hill and get things moving.'

The four ill-assorted people looked at each other, and slow smiles dawned on their faces. Maybe this time they could accomplish something beyond the limited confines of their small world, King thought as they set off toward the main road.

★ ★ ★

Washington Shipp sang in the shower, mostly, but he also sang while driving. He would have been singing on a stage somewhere, after his expensive musical education, if he hadn't discovered that his stage fright was intense and unrelenting enough to make an opera career too painful to contemplate. A switch to criminal justice in mid-college had prepared him to become Templeton, Texas's first black police chief, which was, at times, a very mixed blessing.

As he hit the deep notes of 'Scintille Diamant' from the *Tales of Hoffmann*, he was thinking about the fire he had seen last night. Burning homes was a time-honored tradition among bigwigs in east Texas who intended to control those they considered their lackeys. As far as Wash knew, Ransome Cole had never actually *been* a lackey of the Old Guard, but he had cooperated several times when Wash wouldn't have. Evidently he had stepped on some toes recently, as his words to the fire chief had indicated.

By the process of elimination, the fire was almost certainly involved with the drug case on the river. There were too many odd and unusual circumstances surrounding that situation, anyway. Nothing else going on could have aroused such anger in Nathaniel Farmer, otherwise known as Big Nate.

There had been federal men, narcs and IRS agents all nosing around the county, though not actively in the city limits, and so officially out of Wash's jurisdiction and none of his business. Indeed, he had spoken to that Parker fellow in the courthouse once, and the SOB had all but told Wash he didn't need any local yokels, particularly token black ones, messing in his case. Wash had seen something in the agent's eyes that told him Parker might be put off more than usual by his race.

But Washington Shipp had more than one string to his bow. He'd been raised down in the river bottoms, and only when a flood carried away his daddy's house and a lot of his farmland had they moved to Templeton and taken up yard work. He still had kinfolk down in the low country, and Auntie Libby was only the oldest of the bunch.

It had been Arthur Winchell, rich and prominent and strangely unbigoted, who had discovered Wash's talent, when the boy sang while doing his yard work, and sent him to school. He had understood the stage fright — Arthur had a touch of that himself, it turned out.

Wash could count on quiet information coming in from kin and friends still living near the swamp, or from Holroyd Square, the most influential, if not the wealthiest, part of Templeton. That was where Winchell still lived with his daughter and grandchildren.

Wash intended to do some nosing around of his own, asking questions of those who usually knew what was happening out in the county. He might even make an unobtrusive 'personal' trip to the river country and see young Wim Dooley.

But the first thing he did on arriving at the station was to check the state fire marshal's report on the fire the night before. If it was arson, then it was his business, right and proper. From what he had seen and what the fire chief said, it had been caused by a bomb.

A representative of the Bureau of Alcohol, Tobacco, and Firearms was already on hand when he reached his office. Jack Skeeters was not his favorite person, though minimally more acceptable than Stephen Parker. Skeeters had been somewhat subdued since the Ruby Ridge Waco fiascos that his agency had mishandled so badly. That was all to the good. A Skeeters subdued was much better than one filled with hot air and self-importance.

He nodded to the man as he went into his office. 'Come on in, Jack,' he said over his shoulder. 'I'll be with you just as soon as I look at the incoming. Might be something I need to tend to.'

He knew it bothered Skeeters to have to wait on anybody, and he took great pleasure in going through his pile of overnight reports and sorting them, carefully, into their proper categories. When he turned to Skeeters, the man was chewing ferociously on an unlit cigar. The no-smoking policy did have its good points, he decided.

'I expect you're here about the Cole fire last night,' Wash began. 'It certainly looks like the work of an arsonist, and Ranse saw the car dropping off the man who placed the bomb. We've even got the license number.'

'Stolen,' Skeeters interrupted.

'Of course,' Wash agreed. 'People who do such things tend to take care of details. But Ranse saw the man who threw the bomb, did you know that?'

Skeeters looked interested and tucked the cigar away into his pocket. 'Did he, now.' It wasn't a question. 'He didn't mention that to me.'

Wash sighed. 'Ransome Cole is the sheriff of this county,' he said. 'He doesn't take kindly to being treated like a suspect, and if you used your normal tactics you put his back up right off the bat. Jack, you're a horse's ass, and you can't seem to help showing it. I know you and make allowances, but not everybody does. Ranse has some horse blood, himself, though he isn't near as bad as some sheriffs we've had around here. If you'd gone in and talked with him like a human being, it's surprising what you might have learned.' He leaned back in the deep chair that Chief Rawlinson had worn over thirty years into natural curves that fit a man's body.

'May I remind you,' Skeeters said in a whiney voice that riled Wash considerably, 'that I represent the United States government. You owe me the utmost cooperation and consideration. Nobody insulted the DEA people who were here, or the IRS agent.'

'Well, if I'd had the chance I'd have remedied that,' Wash told him. 'But they ignored me entirely, which suited me just fine. Bunch of educated idiots, thinking that just because things are done one way in Washington, D.C., they have to be the same down here. I have to give you credit, Jack; you know how people think around here, and you're the same arrogant bastard to everybody. There's something to be said for consistency.'

Skeeters might be rude, but he wasn't stupid. He looked faintly gratified as he leaned over the desk and asked, 'What did Cole say about the bomber? We've got our people working on the bomb itself, and before long we'll be able to tell what it was made of — and maybe even who made it.'

Wash got out his personal notebook and read off Cole's words verbatim. 'And that's it,' he concluded. 'But it seems like a good bit. They hadn't a clue that somebody was watching for them, so they didn't take the care they might have, otherwise. And those long arms Cole described — that's the sort of thing people would remember, don't you think?' he asked.

A grin spread across Skeeters' ruddy face. 'It is. My God, it is!' he chortled. 'Solly Campbell, by damn! We got a flyer about him last year, after that big fire in Kansas City. Somebody was sleeping in his car before an important early meeting, and he saw that bastard set the incendiary device in the elevator and send it up. Fellow was sleepy and disoriented, but he had the good sense to crank his car and hightail it out of there, or he might have been trapped when the fire rushed up and down the elevator shaft and set everything off. I'll be damned!

'Who'd have thought we'd come up with a pro like Solly, way down here in the boonies? The organization that hired him owned the building and stood to collect a mint, if the insurance people hadn't balked. The fire people thought the thing was caused by an electrical problem in the elevator's wiring. Good thing the insurers called ATF in, or the crooks would have got away with forty-two million dollars.'

Wash was impressed. Whatever you said about Jack Skeeters, he had a memory like an elephant. As the ATF man left his office, Shipp wondered if he would ever be able to like him, but that was so unlikely that he shrugged it off and got to work on his report.

He had a fire to investigate, and whoever had set it off, it was Wash's job to find the money-man who had paid for it to be done and, behind him, the power broker who had started this odd string of events with his shipment of drugs — drugs and what else? Aunt Libby had told him Wim mentioned something big that he never got details about, and that interested Wash a lot.

Wash had known about many such shipments that had been seized, lost, or stolen, and the kingpins had never seemed to notice much. There was always more where that came from. What was it about this particular shipment that was so special it could trigger so many nasty events?

He'd find out, Wash thought, no matter what it took. A good first step might be a visit to Auntie Libby, down in the low country. She knew everything, just about, and what she didn't know she probably could guess at pretty close. As she had set him on the track, she probably expected a visit along about now, anyway. After that — well, when he was a boy he'd met Lena McCarver. If she remembered him and was in the mood, he might learn something from her. The deep woods was full of information, if you just knew where to look for it.

It was noon before Wash could finish the work waiting for him and get away from his office. He had a lot of unused vacation time, and he signed out for the rest of that day and all of the next. If he didn't use up some of that free time by the end of the year, he knew he'd lose it again, as he had been doing for years now.

His wife Jewel fussed at him frequently for failing to take off and see new country, but he knew she understood his need to do a better job as police chief than anyone else. One day he'd feel he had caught up to Chief Rawlinson, who had given him his chance with the local Force, and then he might take time to go on a cruise or take Jewel to Europe.

Thinking of Jewel, he stopped by the house. She'd likely enjoy riding out with him and seeing the kinfolk, even if they still considered her that 'city girl' (born and raised in Templeton) Wash married.

10

Young William

School had started weeks before, but this was a Saturday. Wim was helping his ma in the fall garden when a dusty car pulled up in the overgrown track leading from the dirt road to the Dooley house. His mother flinched, and he grew angry, remembering the way the government men had treated her before when they came around asking questions.

Worse yet was that Fielding man, who had tried to bully information out of her. Wim had carried the axe out into the side yard, where his mother was backed against the ash tree, pale and shaking, while Fielding yelled and shook her. Only when the axe blade bit into the tree beside his head, to be jerked out quickly and readied again, did Fielding spin around. Wim watched him size up his opposition and decide that confronting a country boy with an axe was not a wise thing to do.

Today, ready to do battle again, the boy turned to face the man who was moving toward them like a large, dark cloud. Then Wim sighed with relief. This was Miz Libby's nephew, Wash Shipp, from town.

'Man wants to talk to me, Ma,' he said over his shoulder as he moved toward the police chief.

'Wim . . . ' Her voice was low, but her tone was a warning.

'Don't worry, Ma. He's not like any of those bastards that came here before. Chief Shipp belongs to Miz Libby. He'll know what's right to do.'

He could see the doubt in her eyes, but she trusted him more than anyone — and she let him go.

'Chief Shipp?' Wim called, and the big man paused, waiting for the boy to reach him at the end of the garden row.

'My auntie told me you needed to talk to me,' Shipp said, smiling.

Wim gestured toward a shade tree in the side yard, where a bench made of a plank set across two saw horses offered a place to sit.

'I've got a cold Coke in the car,' Shipp added. 'You want something to drink?'

Wim nodded. It wasn't often he had the money for a bought soft drink.

Shipp went back to the car, where a cooler provided two ice-sweated red cans. Wim popped the top of his, listening with satisfaction to the *whoosh*. That first icy swallow was wonderful, and Shipp waited until the boy had savored it before speaking.

'Seems you know about something that might be . . . dangerous?' the big man asked at last. 'Something you don't want anybody to know you know?'

Wim nodded, feeling the tickle of the Coke at the back of his throat. 'I get around, down the river, along the creeks, through most of the swamp,' he said. 'There's things go on down there that nobody else knows, 'less it's old Possum Choa — and he never talks to nobody but me and a few others.'

'And you see and hear things when nobody knows you're around,' mused

Shipp. 'I used to do the same, when I was a boy growing up down here. Slipped along in the shallows or lay in the cool fern brakes hearing the birds and whatever else was about. Learned a lot. I bet you do, too.'

'Sure do.' Wim took another sip and sighed. 'I'm friends with old Choa. Between us, we know just about everything that goes on down here. You know that business the Feds were looking into? I know where that box is.'

Shipp sat upright on the plank, staring into Wim's eyes. 'And where is that?'

Wim stared across the road at a buzzard circling high and cool above the forest. 'The sinkhole.' He barely mouthed the words.

Shipp's dark eyes widened. 'The big one? God, boy, nothing ever comes out of there! The Feds would raise a hullabaloo if they knew — and Nate Farmer and his boys . . . whoo-ee! They'd all be mighty upset if they knew.' Shipp leaned back against the nearby tree and took another sip from his red can. 'But as it is, young Wim, they'll never know.'

'They know, all right. Possum saw me home, thinking I didn't know about nothin'. But I followed him back — and I was close by when he led a big fellow down to the sinkhole and showed him where the box went in. Then he let the man go. Showed him the way out, leaving tracks, and broke twigs to mark the way. And we've already had that Fielding man out, trying to make Ma tell him something she don't know anything about. You can bet, Mr. Shipp, that whoever wants that box the worst is going to come back to find it.' The possibilities this opened up made Wim swallow hard.

He could see those possibilities spinning behind Shipp's eyes, as well. They sat still, looking at each other. Then Shipp grunted and rose, holding out his hand.

'You've done a wise thing, Wim,' he said. 'Now don't worry about it anymore, and don't, whatever you do, go back into the swamp for a while. Whatever goes on down there is likely to be very nasty, and so dangerous I'd hate for you to get caught up in it.'

'Ma needs me,' the boy said, his voice

quiet. 'The kids need me, too. I'll stay close to home, Mr. Shipp. I promise.' He spat between two fingers and crossed his heart. 'But you get those critters if you can. Or see they get *got*, if you see what I mean.'

'I do, indeed,' the policeman said. 'And I'll see the right thing done, even if I haven't the authority to do it myself. There's others who can, and will. You just mosey along your way, doing whatever you do naturally, and if anybody asks, you don't know *anything* about *anything*.'

Wim watched as the dust curled after the departing car. That was a good man, he'd always heard. Now he believed it. When he went back to the garden to join his mother, he was whistling under his breath, and the sound made Ma look up and smile with relief.

★　★　★

There had been a tale used by mothers and grandmothers to keep their children in line, down in the brakes when Wash was little. 'If you're not good, we'll call

Miz Lena on you. She'll fix you!' That had been enough to bring even the most rambunctious child into line. Now, as he turned out of the ruts marking the lane into the Dooley place, Wash considered deliberately bearding that little old lady in her den, and he wondered if it wouldn't help to take someone along who knew her and might have some influence with her. He remembered Auntie Libby telling him that Boze Blair had been carrying groceries and such out to the McCarver place for many years. If he could catch Boze at home, maybe the old fellow would go with him to visit the old woman.

He still had childhood visions of a sharp-eyed old lady with strange abilities. His mother's description of Lena had stuck in his mind for over thirty years, he realized, and as he turned off on the oil-top leading to the Blair farm he found himself clenching his teeth.

Wash had known Boze since he was a child. In fact, back when Boze hauled hay for the dairy farmers, who used to be so numerous in Nichayac County, Wash made most of his school money helping him load hay bales in the field and unload them into his neighbors' barns. Even after he went away to college, he'd spent several summers working with the old fellow.

So Boze was a known and comfortable quantity. Wash intended to sound out the old fellow before asking him to go with him to the McCarver place. If anyone down here knew about strangers poking around in the river bottom country, it would be Lena McCarver.

When Wash turned into the long tree-shaded drive, he could see the Blair pickup parked before the arbor vitae bush that flanked the yard gate. He was in luck. Old though he was, Boze stayed busy, if only visiting neighbors or playing dominos in the shade of the oak tree beside the general store.

Today he was sitting in the swing in the side yard under his pecan tree. His lap was full of late fall peas, and he and his wife were shelling them into big pans, dropping the hulls into bushel baskets at their feet. A brindle cow was watching them, her head hung over the lot fence some yards from the scene of action, waiting. Wash grinned. She knew she'd get the hulls, in time, and her mouth was already watering.

He honked politely and got out of the car. Three hound pups came lolloping out from under the arbor vitae and began yipping and growling and worrying his shoelaces.

'Get down now,' the old man yelled at them. 'Come in, Wash, and shell some peas. Bet it's been years since you did that.'

'Not since July, anyway,' Wash said. 'I need some help, Mr. Blair. You mind if I sit down and tell you about it?'

Blair's wife rose and slipped into the house. Wash took her place, picking up her basin of peas and shelling as he talked.

'You know there's been a lot going on down here,' he said. 'Not much of my business, until now. Maybe not altogether my business now, but somebody has burned the sheriff's house in town, and I take that to mean I've been invited to the party.' A rattle of peas hailed into the pan. 'I know nothing much goes on down here that the old-timers don't know about. And Lena McCarver probably knows the most. I want to go see her. I'd like for you to go with me, if you don't mind. I'm still . . . a little in awe of her.'

Boze snorted. 'Well you might be, boy. Well you might! I've knowed that woman for fifty years, and I'm in awe of her, too.' He spat into a clump of ageratum. 'Be glad to go with you, boy. And it's a good thing you come around to me, 'cause Miz Lena has locked her gate and hid her road. But she give me a key to her gate, long years back. She just now sent me a note to tell me to bring it along next time I fetch her groceries. So we're all fixed up. You let me set all this junk down, and I'll get my hat and the key. We'll be on our way in just a jiffy.'

Watching the old fellow hobble up the back steps into the house, Wash marveled at the way country people lasted. They might get skinny and weathered, reddened and wrinkled by sun, but they hung in there, tough as old roots, until something big and tough and nasty finally carried them off. It looked as if Boze might last for a good few years more.

The roads were dusty, for it hadn't rained in weeks. Bumping over the dirt tracks had Wash's head aching long before he reached the gap into the McCarver place. At that point he stopped and stared, while beside him Boze chuckled.

The cattle guard was invisible from the main road, and the metal gate seemed overgrown with berry vines. If Boze had not assured him that this was the place, he'd have thought this a long-abandoned lane, impossible to travel.

Boze got out and pushed through the vines to the gate, where he fumbled for the rusty lock. He struggled with it for several minutes, without success. Even when Wash lent his great strength to the task, he had to back off or break the key inside the lock.

Boze looked up at him, his watery gray eyes solemn. 'Miz Lena don't want comp'ny, it's plain to see. When I come with her groceries nex' week, I'll bet that sucker opens up slick as a weasel.'

'Likely you're right,' Wash agreed. He climbed out of the vines and got back into his dusty car. 'I just wish I could find some way to figure out what's going on down here. I have a feeling things are about to rip, but God only knows how and when.'

Boze spat a long streak of tobacco juice out of the window. 'You want to know about the low country, you go find that boy Wim, down t'other side of the swamp. If you could find old Possum, he could tell you what you want to know, but nobody ever finds Possum Choa 'less he wants you to. Wim, though, is young and cur'ous and would love to be in on any excitement. You go talk to that boy.'

Wash didn't admit he had already done that and warned the boy to stay clear of the swamp. But he realized Boze was right. If he intended to learn what he needed to know, he had to go back, eat crow, and invite the youngster into the game that was, he felt with increasing certainty, already being played out by known and unknown participants.

* ★ *

Back during the Depression, when his father had worked the family's cotton farm, wearing only his raincoat in order to save his only good pair of hickory stripe overalls for trips to town, Nate Farmer had promised himself that he would have *money* before he died. However it had to be done, he had sworn a Bible oath to see after his mother and sisters and to own land and cattle and big cars and good clothes — if he had to walk over bodies to do it.

And he'd done all of it, leaving quite a few bodies along the way. Not that he ever dirtied his hands with that kind of mess — he had specialists to tend to such matters, and ordinarily they did a good job.

Now, leaning back in his leather chair, behind his impressive desk, he stared into the face of his second-in-command. 'Harland, you're not doin' the *job*,' he complained.

Fielding turned pale. Those exact words had preceded more than one disappearance. He knew that for a fact, having been there a few of those times. The men involved had been shot and buried deep in the woods.

'Nate, I've done everythin' I can,' he said, barely keeping his voice under control.

Nate considered the uncomfortable Harland. He'd never bothered to slick himself up in any way. It wasn't how you talked, he'd decided decades ago, that made the difference. It was how you *thought* that either put you on top or on the bottom. And now this smartass dude had been dumped at his gate like a bag of garbage. No way would Nate Farmer put up with that kind of insult.

There were still suits up in Templeton who thought he was an ignorant redneck they could fool and cheat. They wouldn't learn any different if they checked out his bank accounts and tax returns, either. There were experts who could hide money slick as a whistle, with no evidence it ever existed, much less where it came from.

The drug business was profitable. The

lesser projects scattered around the county were income, though not *big* income. But this last deal had been the biggest he'd ever attempted, and if he didn't come through with that *thing* hidden in the middle of the missing ice chest, he might well pay it off with his own blood. Dead men had no use for money.

Farmer sighed. 'Harland, we've got a problem here that's goin' to take a lot of fixin'. You sure and certain none of them folks down around the river knows how to find Possum Choa?

'Oscar said plain and clear the old man's the one that put the chest in that sinkhole. We've had men out there pokin' and pryin' into every bit of quicksand we can locate, but that damn swamp's an almighty big place. We got to find that black Injun and make him take us to it.'

Fielding shook his head. 'They all swear that nobody *ever* found the old man's place except that lost deputy, and he couldn't find it again when he tried. And that Dooley woman don't hardly know her own name. The painter woman,

Irene Follette, tried to smart-mouth me, and I hit her a good one and left her lyin' flat. Old Lena — well, I don't think even you'd want to try messin' with her any more.'

Nate closed his eyes, leaned back in the leather chair, and thought hard. He had flown over the river bottom country fifteen years back, looking for likely transfer points for his drug runners. Things showed up from the air . . .

He sat up, cursing himself for being so old-fashioned. 'How 'bout we hire one of them helicopters and search from the air? Oscar said that was the biggest sinkhole he ever seen in his life, and he was born down there. One that big ought to show up like a sore thumb, don't you think?'

Fielding narrowed his eyes and nodded slowly. 'Have to be careful about how we do it, Nate. Don't want anybody to suspect what we're up to, do we?'

Farmer shook his head impatiently. 'My nephew up to Tyler has one he bought from Army Surplus. Uses it for sprayin' his fields. That chest couldn't weigh more than maybe fifteen, twenty

215

pounds. Should be plenty of lift there. And Grady knows how to keep his mouth shut — he better, 'cause I started him off in business and hold his notes.'

The idea excited him now, and he picked up the phone and punched buttons. 'Grady? Uncle Nate. Got a little job for you — you still got that chopper?'

In two minutes he had his nephew on the move. The machine would be on his farm tomorrow by ten o'clock, Grady assured him.

Farmer turned to Fielding. 'You go down to the marina and get some heavy-duty grapplin' stuff. Hooks, nets, cables — the whole shebang. We'll go in low, just above the trees, and spy out the land. Shouldn't take more'n two, three days to scout the area Oscar showed us. Then we'll go in late in the evenin' and dredge every sinkhole we can find. With a powerful metal detector, we ought to be able to find what we want.'

'That chest was aluminum,' Fielding objected.

'What's in it *ain't*,' Nate responded.

'We'll take a Geiger counter, too, just in

case. Between 'em, we'll get that sucker out of there, and Possum Choa be damned.'

★ ★ ★

Wim Dooley was a boy of his word. When he promised Chief Shipp that he'd stay close to home, he meant it; except for school, he stayed right there, keeping an eye on his ma and the children and wondering desperately what was going on. He had a pretty good idea what that Fielding fellow had been looking for when he came to the Dooley place. Choa had let that drug runner go, and he must have told his bosses where the ice chest was. Nobody but Choa could find it, except for Wim, and it was clear that the grown-ups would never guess he knew anything.

Only Shipp had consulted him, and it bothered him a lot that he'd been fettered this way. He felt just like the young steer they'd tied to a stake in the pasture; he'd like to do some snorting and pawing himself, just from pure frustration.

He was out in the fall garden Saturday morning, planting a fresh batch of turnip greens, when he heard a sound that had always fascinated him. Sometimes the narcs checked the low country in a chopper, looking for stands of marijuana, and this sounded much the same — yet in some way it was different, too. The engine had a different pitch and the blades seemed to make more of a whine when the thing went over, very low, beyond the potato field.

His mother came out of the house and looked up, shading her eyes with one calloused hand. 'What you s'pose they want, Wim? They're a lot lower than they ought to be.'

Wim struggled mightily with his conscience and lost. 'I'll just follow along off to the side and see which way they go,' he told her. 'Looks like they're searchin' for somethin'. Might be somebody lost in the swamp.'

He could see the idea take hold of her. Ma felt as if she was responsible for everybody, and she nodded. 'You find out. If help's needed, you run back and get me.'

Wim dashed away through the cut-over wood flanking the river bottoms. Though the chopper was out of sight, its distinctive sound guided him after it, and he soon realized that once it was over the southern edge of the swamp it had begun to make regular sweeps, east to west.

'They're lookin' for that hole where we put the chest,' he muttered to himself. 'Sure as shootin' . . . '

He could tell from the sound that they were a long way from the site of the sinkhole. It would take them all day. But tomorrow they would get closer.

'I've got to get word to Chief Shipp,' he said aloud. 'Possum'll keep an eye on that thing, but I bet the law ought to know it's down here.'

The chopper came into view on the near leg of its sweep, so low it seemed about to brush the tops of the trees. Sheltered under a thick pine, Wim stared, shading his eyes, studying the craft, memorizing the identification numbers on its tail. That might be something the chief could use. Then he turned and dashed for home. If he hopped it, he could maybe make it to Miz Libby's by taking the shortcut through the pine flats.

His ma looked apprehensive when he pounded up, but she seemed to read serious purpose in his eyes. 'What's wrong, Wim?'

'That chopper's no gover'ment one, Ma. It's goin' back and forth across the low country, and Chief Shipp needs to know about it. Kin I run to Miz Libby's and get her to send word to him?' His face felt as if it were about to burst, and his heart was galloping like a runaway horse.

'You git you a drink of water first, boy. You look like a ripe tomato. Then you kin take off for Miz Libby's. But don't run yourself totally to death.'

It was shady in the pine flats, and Wim jogged along, letting himself cool a bit. Only when he came to the long ridge separating the brakes from the bottoms did he begin to hurry again. Something inside told him this was important, and he had to move fast.

When he came through the thin swatch of cane alongside the dirt road that bisected the brakes, he slowed again and turned into the lane leading to the old woman's shady yard. By now it was almost noon, and the smell of black-eyed peas and cornbread wafted from the back door as the boy stepped onto the porch.

He tapped softly on the screen door frame. 'Miz Libby? You there?' His mouth was watering, for Wim was always hungry.

A halting step inside told him she was coming to the door. 'Why, Wim Dooley! You come right in here, child, and drink you some ice tea. You had your lunch yet? Boys is always hungry, so you set right down at this table. I hate to eat alone. Lucy Bee, down the road, cooked me up this dinner, but she couldn't stay to share it with me.' The old woman brought another plate from her shelf and set a fork beside it, then groaned her way down into a splint-bottomed chair and grinned at him. 'You need to get in touch with Wash? I thought you might. But first we get rid of some of this here grub.'

When they were finished he helped Libby clear the table, and washed the dishes in her old-fashioned porcelain sink. After things were tidy again, she sat him down and questioned him closely. When he had told her all he knew, she nodded.

'You're right, Wim. Wash ought to know there's a 'copter checking out the swamp. He can likely find out who it belongs to, from the numbers, too. I'll get Lucy Bee to drive me to the store so I can call him. The telephone my chillun put in here for me don't work today, but that's no problem. Lucy won't mind. Now you run back home — no, I don't mean full tilt. You go home slow enough so you don't fall out with the heat. I'll tell Wash to be sure to go by and see you when he comes.'

Wim looked her in the eye. 'You *sure* he'll come?' he asked.

Libby nodded her neatly kerchiefed head, and her big gold earrings swung. 'You can bet on that,' she said. 'I'll see to it.'

Reassured, Wim turned back toward home. This time, filled with peas and cornbread, he couldn't have run if he tried.

11

A Thief in the Swamp

Nate Farmer was up before dawn, waiting impatiently for the helicopter to arrive. He'd always been fascinated by flying machines, though he never considered going up in one, of any description.

This time he knew he had to go aloft. If the chest was spotted, he had to be on hand. There in the swamp, it would be easy to get rid of any unwanted witnesses, and if he needed to he could ride out in the chopper and 'eliminate' the pilot later. His nephew would understand.

The contact man for the nameless owner of the contraband cargo had called him late the night before, and he had made it clear that nobody involved in the transfer of the shipment would survive its permanent loss. From Oscar Parmelee to Nathaniel Farmer, the entire organization would be eliminated. The thought made

Nate feel cold to the bone. Fielding's run-in with the people down in the bottomlands wouldn't amount to a hill of burned beans compared to what would happen to his own hide. He'd seen things happen that made even his reptilian blood run cold.

Even he had no idea who was at the head of the organization he had been dealing with over the years, smuggling 'extras' in along with drug shipments. Concealed behind a maze of intermediaries, the principals had remained nameless and faceless. He had no handle on the Bosses, and there was no way to strike first, before they had a chance to get him. Hell, he might have one of their agents working for him, right now!

They were a big outfit; he'd known that from the beginning. When his own people had had no luck tracing calls or identifying principals, even when using their contacts in government and the military, he understood what he had gotten into. It was his own fault, Nate knew, but it didn't make him any happier.

He nibbled at his toast, sipped his

coffee, and declined his usual eggs and sausage. He'd heard of air sickness, and he didn't care about upchucking all over himself in mid-air.

He went out into the cool September morning, smelling the fall tang on the breeze. In the horse-lot, he checked hooves, coats, and teeth automatically, but his attention was on the sky above his farm. When the thud-thud-thud of the chopper's rotors sounded, he gave a sigh of relief. Amid the swirling grit of its landing, he shielded his eyes and moved cautiously toward the idling craft.

'Keep clear of the rotors!' Antonio, the pilot, yelled, and he ducked low and ran to the open hatchway.

'*Buenas días*,' Nate said to Antonio. 'My nephew didn't come?'

'No, señor. He have the fall work to do, preparing the fields. He send me to help you all you want. He also send the metal-finder that you ask to use.'

That was good. Nobody would miss Antonio if he had to off him. His nephew was discreet, and he'd never mention having loaned this thing to his old uncle down in the low country. And if his pilot went missing, that was just too bad.

'You got *gasolina*?' the pilot asked. 'We need *mucho*, if we search for long time.'

That was one thing he'd been warned about, and Nate gestured toward the skid tank his truck had deposited beside the fence the night before. 'All you want is right there. I guess we'll have to come back often for a refill?'

'*Sí!*' The pilot dropped from the hatch and ran to uncoil the hose from the tank. While he refilled the chopper, Nate returned to the kitchen and picked up the food and the water jug his housekeeper had prepared for him. He also slipped his .38 into his jacket pocket, just in case. Whoever might be messing around in the swamp today was going to be mighty unlucky if he saw something he shouldn't.

By the time Nate got back to the pasture, Antonio was again in his seat, waiting, his dark face enigmatic. They took off, leaving a cloud of dust behind, and sped toward the east, staying low enough to keep their visibility down, but high enough to stay clear of the trees.

Below, the asphalt roads turned to gravel, then wound and branched and finally became a scanty pattern of dirt tracks between overgrown fields and increasingly large patches of forest. He could see people in the brakes moving around, some working in their fall gardens, some just idling in their front yards waiting for rides to their logging jobs. Over the ridge and beyond a pine flat he recognized the hard-scrabble place that belonged to the Dooleys, with a small shape stooped over a garden row.

High-headed woman! Much to his disgust, she'd kept her brood together, clean and respectable. That young 'un of hers, Wim, was too bright for his own good. Kept an eye on the river and the woods. That boy better not come snooping into his business, Nate thought.

The pilot seemed to know his business. He skimmed the treetops, seeming to feel his position with his hands, because he was watching the forest, the occasional fields, the swampy spots, and the thick gray-green mats of reeds and waterweed slide past. On his own side, Nate squinted downward, amazed at the difference in the terrain from what he saw when standing on the ground.

Anyone could hide in a pine thicket and remain unseen from someone in the sky, he had thought. But that was wrong, for he could see down through the dark green needles to spot a cow grazing in the shade, a dog lying on his stomach, even a dozen white chickens pecking around a scraped-bare yard completely shaded by umbrella chinaberry trees.

Their sweep was methodical, and he found it much slower than he would have thought. There were miles and miles of low country, some of it impassable swamp and brushy tangle, some of it cut-over woods and brier vines, and some of it scabby-looking cornfields overgrown with bindweed. So early in the morning, he saw the occasional deer, fleeing from the noise of the chopper. The few roads, logging tracks, and even footpaths shone white in the sunlight, as if marked out in neon. Not a vehicle was in sight — logging was concentrated further south, in the big flats along the river.

Once he saw a little black boy trudging along a path, a cane pole over his shoulder. When he heard the chopper, he glanced up and then darted into the brush. Another time, Nate spotted two sandy-colored red wolves loping along a stream-bed, flipping bright beads of water about their bodies. He could see sparks of light caught in the droplets in the instant it took to pass over them, and he found it in him to marvel at actually seeing those rare animals running free.

Late September in east Texas can be hot. The sun rose higher, and they were too low to take advantage of the cooling effect of altitude. Nate found himself sweating as they turned and stared, turned and stared. When Antonio called for a fuel break he was more than ready.

So far he had seen nothing that might have been the infamous sinkhole. Even as a boy he had never seen it, and he wondered if Oscar might be lying about what the old man told him.

Then he discarded the notion. There was too much to lose, and Oscar was right in the firing zone. No, the place had to be there. It only took a lot of looking to find it.

*   *   *

Wim returned to help Ma in the garden, but he was antsy at staying so close to home when he could occasionally hear the distant sound of the helicopter's blades. If only Wash Shipp would come! Then he might let Wim go with him to watch the chopper from some hiding place deep in the woods.

He continued to help his mother pull the tough and prickly weeds from around the collards that would supply them with green stuff all winter. By noon he was almost frantic with impatience, but at last Ma headed for the house and lunch.

The children were playing in the sandy yard, tended by Susie and Ella, the oldest of Wim's sisters. They headed for the well and a good washing-up when they saw the gardeners returning. Wim joined them at the washtub and splashed heavenly cool water over his face and shoulders.

There were cold field peas left from the

231

night before, kept from spoiling by being let down into the well in a tight-lidded can. Along with cold cornbread and fresh tomatoes, they filled the growling gap in his belly. Even as he ate, he listened for the sound of a car coming down the road.

It was Ma's firm rule that nobody worked in the heat right after eating, so the entire family found cool spots to nap, either flat on the smooth pine floor of the central hallway in the house, or in the dust of the deep shade under the umbrella chinaberry trees. As Wim lay there, batting at an occasional fly and thinking hard, there came a distant rumble as a car moved along the rough road. Chief Shipp!

He rose and tiptoed among his sleeping kin to the edge of the porch, where his mother was stretched out in the swing, sleeping with her mouth open.

'Ma! Ma, I think Chief Shipp's coming. Kin I go with him, if he takes off to see what that chopper's doin'?' he asked in a whisper.

'Mmm-hmmm,' she sighed, without waking fully, as he had hoped she would.

That was all the permission he intended to get. He scampered up the road, hoping to meet the car before it reached the house and woke his mother completely. It was the dusty black one the chief drove, all right. It pulled to a halt beside the panting boy and Shipp leaned out.

'Wim? What's up, boy? You all right?'

'You see the chopper that's been goin' back and forth across the bottoms?' Wim asked. 'It's been gone for a while, but it spent the whole entire mornin' lookin' for somethin'.'

Shipp opened the door. 'You get in here where it's cool and tell me about it. We'll go back to the brakes to the store and get something cold to drink while you do that, okay?'

As they turned onto a track leading into a cornfield and headed back up the road, Wim described the helicopter and its activities. The chief listened with flattering attention and nodded from time to time as he spoke.

When he was done, Shipp turned in at the store and stopped the engine. 'How

233

far down toward the river is that sinkhole, Wim?' he asked. 'Will they make it that far today?'

Wim thought hard. He had timed the sweeps by his inner clock, which was seldom wrong, and it seemed to him it might be pretty far into the next day before it could possibly cover all the area between its last lap and the hole in which he had helped Possum sink the ice chest.

'If they go like they did today — I could hear the noise every time they come this way — they ought to come nigh the spot tomorrow afternoon sometime, if they work on Sunday. But I wouldn't bet on that, 'cause I might be wrong.'

'Tell you what,' Shipp said. 'If they haven't got further than that today, you're likely right that it'll be tomorrow. I'll come back and get you about ten o'clock, just to make sure we're in plenty of time, if you think you can work us down into the area before they line up with the sinkhole. That all right?'

Wim thought about Ma. Would she let him go? Then he realized that this was one of the few people in the county she

234

trusted, mainly because he was Miz Libby's nephew.

'Fine with me,' he replied. 'I'll be ready. It may be a long time, though. Better bring some bug stuff — I notice most folks hate being et up by mosquitoes. And maybe some sandwiches?' His tone was a bit wistful, though he tried to control it. Peas and cornbread stuck to your ribs all right, but they sure got old after a while.

Shipp grinned. 'It's a date. Now we'll take you back so you can help your ma some more. But we'll get something cold to drink first. And we'll get enough for your brothers and sisters, too. Kind of a treat.'

All the way back home, Wim nursed his can of red soda in one hand and the sack of cold containers holding his siblings' treat in the other. They would sure and certain be surprised and pleased, he knew. And Ma could never refuse to let him go now. She'd feel beholden to Chief Shipp. Even to the extent of letting him miss church? He turned to Shipp.

'Would you mind askin' her yourself?' he inquired. 'For you, she might not fuss if I missed goin' to meetin' with the family.'

Shipp nodded. When they pulled up under the sweetgums in the yard, he got out and approached Ma, and when she got over her astonishment, she agreed to let her son show him the way he needed to find. Even on a Sunday.

'But we ain't going to make a habit of this, you understand,' she said firmly. 'Just this once, as a favor to Miz Libby's nephew.'

★ ★ ★

When he heard the distant *whup-whup* of a helicopter on Saturday, Choa figured he knew what it signified. It was time he looked at what was going on, but first he needed to talk to Lena again. A full-fledged plan had come to him in a dream the night before, and he needed to borrow her rifle to make it workable. He headed out toward her place, now able to make short-cuts across marshy areas that had formerly been too wet to risk.

He got there quickly, because he

hustled his old bones, and when he looked over the ridge he could see Lena sitting on her front steps, Lone beside her, staring up at him. She was too far away for him to read her expression, but the alertness of her position told him she had some idea what might be going on.

By the time he was halfway down the hill, she was coming to meet him, which was not her usual custom. He hurried forward and they went back together toward the porch, where Lone sat regally regarding them.

'Something's about to pop, Possum,' she said. 'Boze and someone else came to my gate yesterday, but I didn't let 'em come in. Now I'm sorry I didn't. There's a disturbance out in the bottomlands, and I have a feeling it has to do with what brought 'em out here.'

'Prob'ly,' Choa said. He dropped to sit in the rickety chair and fanned himself with his hand. 'Gettin' too old to hurry like that,' he said. 'But you're right. There's a chopper searchin' the swamp country, and I'd bet my life it's Farmer, huntin' for his ice chest.'

She began to grin. 'Think it's time I had me another look-see,' she said.

He leaned forward. 'Wait a bit. I got somethin' to tell you that we kin use. Back when I was young, I went into the army, you recall?'

She frowned, and he could see her hunting back through her long memory. Then she nodded. 'True, but you wasn't gone but a few months. Then you come back and nobody knew why.'

'They decided I wasn't military material,' he said, in a good imitation of the starchy tone of the psychiatrist who examined him after he refused to obey stupid or dangerous commands. 'Said if I got crazy orders I was as like to shoot my officer as I was the enemy, which was just about right. But I did learn some stuff that may be useful. Did you know that if a chopper's blades stop, it's goin' to fall? And if the blades can't whirl around the other way to slow its fall, it'll come down like a rock?'

She shook her head slowly, her eyes narrowing as she considered the notion.

'So if somethin' should sort of accidentally freeze up the blades, that sucker would come right down wherever it was.' Her grin grew broad. 'And whoever is in it would come down, too.'

'A high-powered rifle can do the job,' he said, nodding, '*if* you know what to shoot at — and I do. But my old gun has seen its best days. Seems like I recall you got yourself a real nice rifle a while back. Might be I could borrow it?' He felt a bit shy about asking such a thing, for a gun was a mighty personal item, and most people didn't like to loan them out.

Lena cocked her head and slanted her black eyes at him, reminding him of a wren on a branch. She nodded slowly, as if considering everything, then jerked her chin toward the tumbledown house.

'You come right in and let me get that gun. I'll give you some extra cartridges, too. You get to be our age, you don't always hit what you aim at, the first pop out of the box.'

Though he lacked at least a decade of equaling Lena's age, Choa agreed as he followed her in, wondering if he *would* need more than one shot — or if he'd even have the chance to get off more than one shot. A chopper could scat out of range mighty fast, he recalled.

The ancient hardwood floors creaked under his feet as he moved across the kitchen to the rack Lena had put up over her window. She stretched up to reach it and brought down a gem of a gun, although not by any means a new one.

'A 1903 Springfield,' Choa sighed. 'Prime shape, too. That gun, Miz Lena, might've been used in the First World War. Send a slug that should bring down that machine, if I hit a blade just right.'

She stared up at him, her eyes bright as jet in the dim light. 'You've got somethin' else in mind besides just bringing it down. I can see it in your eye, Possum Choa. I've got a funny feeling about this. You be careful, you hear me?'

He said nothing, just nodded. He took a while to practice with the gun, just to make sure he knew how its sight was set. Way out there at Lena's, there was nothing to hit but trees, and he hauled up a makeshift target by the rope that raised

Lena's signal in the big pine tree.

She sat on the porch, reassuring her tomcat, while he got the feel of the gun and hit the strip of plywood five times out of six. He only missed the first shot. After that he aimed a bit lower than seemed right and hit every one solidly after that.

'Good,' Lena called to him. 'You're ready. Take a pocket full of ammunition, now, and keep your own head down. There's few enough of us old-timers left down here. Can't afford to lose any of us.'

Choa wrapped the rifle in a gunny-sack and dropped the finger-sized cartridges into his pockets, where they made his pants feel as if they were about to fall off. Clinking together, they made his walk homeward noisier than he liked.

By the time he reached the big creek leading into the swamp, he could hear the irritable whirr of the chopper, and that reassured him. They were still a good distance from the sinkhole. It would be Sunday before they could get that far.

A good night's sleep wouldn't hurt. His bones ached, now that the nights were cooling down and the blackgums were beginning to show bright scarlet leaves amid their dark green crests. It was a good long hike to the sinkhole from his cabin, and he appreciated the chance to think about what he would do when he approached his goal.

He woke only when a mockingbird began tuning up outside. He grunted to his feet and stepped onto the rickety porch to look up at the stars. There was no sign of dawn, but it wasn't more than an hour off. Time to move, he decided.

He slung the rifle, now protected by his own ancient leather gun-case, over his shoulder by the sling, stuck a couple of cold potatoes left over from supper into his pocket, and headed for his dock. There was a short-cut this time of year by way of a tangle of deep creeks that were now filling with the early fall rains. He could paddle his way toward his goal for several miles before taking to the trails.

He hated to think about what he intended to do. His people had never shrunk from killing, but they had seldom gone out of their way to do it, either. Why didn't the white men tend to their own business in their own places and leave these wild spots alone? He'd never figured that out. Just as soon as they found a wonderful place, full of growing things and fish to catch and game to trap, they had to build roads to it and ramps for power boats and houses to keep the weather off. Then they weren't satisfied with it because they'd ruined everything they came there to find. There was just no figuring them.

An hour after sunrise he began to hear the *whup-whup* of the chopper again.

By the time he pulled his boat into a clump of cattails and hid it, the thing had settled into a regular pattern, and he could just about time its arrival at the sinkhole. If they had sensitive detection devices, they'd surely spot that whatever-it-might-be in the ice chest — but he'd be there first.

12

The Watchers in the Woods

Wash wasn't surprised to find Wim waiting out on the road when he bumped up the iron-hard ruts and stopped. He leaned to open the passenger-side door. 'Hop in, Wim. How far can we go in the car before we have to walk? And can we get there before the chopper does?'

Wim thought for a moment. 'Go back up the road a quarter mile and take that wagon track that leads off toward the northeast. It'll take us as near as we can get without walkin'.'

If the washboard road to Wim's house was bad, this track was much worse. Used mainly by wagons pulled by mules or tractors, it wandered around stumps, through clumps of sassafras sprouts, and finally into the big woods, twisting to miss huge magnolias and oaks and ash trees.

Wash was here to catch a criminal,

whether or not it was his business or in his jurisdiction. He didn't want the sheriff or the Feds or anybody else messing around in his own part of the county and bothering people they thought they could bully.

'You think there's any way to get that ice chest out of the sinkhole?' Wim asked. 'Seems to me that nobody would ever in the world be able to find it — much less raise it up again.'

'If they've got a helicopter,' Wash said, 'then they've probably got equipment that could find it. If the thing's radioactive, that might be pretty easy to do. And the navy's got stuff that can let you pick up almost anything off the bottom of the sea, if you pinpoint it first.'

They jounced along in silence for a long time, winding deeper and deeper into the low country. When the track finally ended at a turn-around circling a magnolia tree at least eight feet in diameter, Wash killed the engine.

Together the two listened hard. The chopper was a dim disturbance in the distance. After a while it became more distant, until they couldn't hear it at all.

'You s'pose they've given up?' Wim asked.

'No. I'd bet they had to go back for more fuel,' Wash said. 'Let's get out and hot-foot it to the sinkhole while there's time. I'd like to be there the first time they fly close to it. That'll tell us if they have any of that fancy gear.'

Wash pulled his backpack from the rear seat and shrugged his arms through the straps. Wim looked at him questioningly. 'We'll need water, something to eat, maybe even a snakebite kit or something of the sort. We don't know how long we're going to be here, now do we?'

There was a dim track leading off toward the east, but Wim didn't take it. Instead, he ducked beneath a thicket of yaupon bushes that seemed to form a solid wall, and Wash had to bend double to follow him. That close to the ground, he could see a path made by small animals as they went about their business in the forest. Watching the path was like taking a census of the creatures living down here in the bottomland, he thought.

When he could straighten his back again he found that now they were in the clean-floored wood beneath the great trees. There were a few pines, monsters that would have filled loggers mad with greed; but as Wash followed Wim deeper between the trees, they became fewer. The ground here was too wet for them.

Wim was as silent as an Indian. Even Possum Choa couldn't have heard him coming. Wash was no slouch in the woods — he'd been a boy down here himself. He knew his way around, but he had lost the knack for absolute silence, he found, while stomping around town in boots.

It seemed that they moved through the trees for a long time, following first one path, then another, none of them made by human feet. The sun now began to cast shafts of light through chinks in the overhead canopy, and the birds had tuned up even louder. Squirrels scampered among the oaks and the occasional hickories, gathering their winter store of nuts. So far was this wood from the usual haunts of people that they weren't afraid; they sat on branches, fluffy tails flicking nervously, while scolding the intruders as they passed.

'You ever squirrel hunt down here?' Wash asked.

'Got no gun. Even if I did, though, I wouldn't hunt squirrels. Not enough meat on 'em.' Then the boy paused, listening. The chopper had been back for some time, but now it sounded much closer than before.

'How long?' Wash asked. 'We going to be in time?'

Wim gauged the angle of a sunbeam and nodded. 'Just about. This way, now, and be careful. There's snakes around the sinkhole. You got on boots, which is good, but some of them big moccasins can strike higher than that. Step mighty careful!'

Wash looked down at the boy's tough bare feet. 'Wim, what about you? It's dangerous to go without anything on your feet.'

The boy laughed. 'Lord, Chief Shipp, snakes pay no heed to me. I kin slip up on a moccasin and grab it behind the head, if I want. Somehow they don't seem to see me.'

He'd heard of such things, Wash recalled from his boyhood. There were people who could handle snakes, catch wild birds with their hands, call animals to them. If Wim was one such, he was truly blessed, but it still made him nervous to think about those bare feet.

Before they had gone far, the ground became soft underfoot, then squishy. A long gray-brown shape slithered off into the brush ahead of Wash, making his skin crawl. Yet Wim's brown feet stepped unhesitatingly over turtles and around snakes until they stopped in a tangle of rattan vines and hawthorn bushes. Overhead, bamboo formed a roof dense enough to hide them, even from a low-flying chopper.

'Right here's where I aimed for. Gives us a look at the sinkhole without getting out where anybody might see us,' Wim said, raising his voice to be heard above the increasing noise of the helicopter.

Wash crouched beside the boy, after

checking the vicinity for moccasins and copperheads. He unstrapped his back-pack and took out a pair of binoculars. With the thick growth, there was little chance of the lenses reflecting sunlight to warn the searchers that they were being watched.

From time to time he scanned slowly from right to left, and as the chopper followed its search pattern it came into his field of vision at last. It was obviously army surplus, and still painted with camouflage, but its engine sounded steady and businesslike. The pilot was clearly well-trained, for the machine skimmed the forest's canopy closely, following the contours of the treetops, yet remaining clear of obstructions.

The sinkhole was an anonymous gray-green spot that looked almost like a muddy clearing. The skim of water over its top grew an irregular layer of algae, which Wash knew would look like grass from the air. Would the pilot know that this was a likely place to investigate?

He could hear Wim's heart thumping fast and as he glanced down he saw the boy leaning forward, his gaze fixed on the approaching aircraft. Wash felt his own heart begin to pick up its pace as the mottled shape came closer and closer. When it turned from its regular pattern to hover over the sinkhole, they both let out the breath they had been holding unconsciously.

'The game is going to take the bait,' Wash muttered.

Wim shook his head. 'I never count on that till I got my hands on the critter,' he said.

The chopper came down lower, its blades stirring up a commotion among the surrounding branches and pushing the algae aside to show the murky water beneath it. A dark object appeared, hanging from a cable and stabilized by two smaller lines, one on either side.

As the chopper hung there, Wash found himself wondering what sort of detector that might be. Was the hidden object in that ice chest radioactive? Would the device be sensitive enough to locate it under all the gunk that filled the sinkhole? Deliberately, he inhaled and exhaled, and found to his amusement that Wim was doing the same.

Suddenly, an ear-splitting *crack* exploded through the trees, echoing in his head as he watched unbelievingly. The chopper dropped like a stone into the quagmire, one blade angled strangely and seeming to try to turn around its rotor shaft. But before it could do that, the chopper splashed into the gunk below it and sank. Someone dove out of the open hatch from which the detector had dangled, but the top of the hatch caught him in the back as the chopper went down like a rock, taking its passengers with it.

'God!' Wash gasped, and he felt Wim huddled against his side, trembling.

'Is there any way to get 'em out?' Wim asked in a shaky voice.

'If we had a winch and a float and several men to help us, plus a tractor or two, we might get the wreckage out,' Wash told him. 'Nobody would be alive by the time anybody could get to them, though. By now they're down there with the deer skeletons, the bears and bobcats, and surely a million turtles and such that have gone down for a thousand years or more. Did you ever hear of anybody even trying to get something *out* of there?'

'Far as I know, only me 'n' Possum Choa even know where it is,' the boy said. 'Nobody else ever comes here.'

Wash began to stand up but stopped abruptly, putting out a hand to keep Wim down, too. Beyond the sinkhole, in the shadows of the trees, a dim shape moved toward the edge of the hole. It carried a rifle, which it leaned against a cypress before going to the very edge of the morass.

Wash reached for his sidearm, but Wim grabbed his arm. 'That's Possum Choa,' he said. 'He put that thing there, and he made sure nobody ever got it out again. Seems fair to me, since there's nothin' anybody could do for those men, anyway.'

Wash sank back on his heels, thinking hard. All his instincts told him that he had seen murder done. Yet his head also told him that at least one of the men in that craft had caused murder to be done hereabouts for many years, using the hands of others to pull triggers and wield tire irons and do other even more cruel things to those he wanted dead or terrified.

It wasn't law, but it was rough justice of a sort, he supposed, as he rose and stepped into the narrow strip of open ground that edged the sinkhole. Across the troubled ripples, now settling again into smoothness that was occasionally troubled by a burp of escaping air from beneath the surface, the shooter looked into his face.

So this was Possum Choa, Wash thought, and he shivered at finally meeting the legendary hermit. The old man had lived down here most of his life, and he was protecting his own turf, it was clear. Wash couldn't find it in him to blame him.

'Was that Nate Farmer?' he called to the man beyond the hole.

The deep voice rumbled in response. 'I 'spect so. He found out where his stuff was, *whatever* it was, and he couldn't let it rest. Had to get his hands on it or die. You kin see he died tryin'.' The old man shrugged. 'You going to arrest me and take me in for killin' him?' he asked.

Washington Shipp shrugged in turn. 'You didn't shoot any*body*. Far as I can tell, you shot a *thing*, not a man. No law against shootin' machinery that I know about. At least not down here in the bottomlands.'

Choa grinned, his teeth a pale flash in his dark face. 'Then I'll go on home now,' he said. He stepped back and caught up the rifle. Then, like some spirit of the swamp, he disappeared among the shadowy tree trunks.

Shipp looked down into Wim's eyes, which were wide in his pale, freckled face. 'We had us a fishing trip today, Wim, don't you agree? Came down here to fish, got ourselves lost, and wandered around almost all day finding our way out again. I've got my pole and tackle box in the trunk of the car, in case anybody asks. Did you see anything unusual?'

Wim's color had begun to come back, and his eyes lost their worried look. 'Didn't see a thing except critters and birds,' he said.

They smiled at each other as they

turned to wriggle their way back into the shelter of the big trees. As far as Wash could see, Choa had saved the county a big batch of money — without costing the taxpayers a dime.

★ ★ ★

Ransome Cole was feeling pretty good. Mae was staying with her sister Ellen while he fixed up their damaged house and put it on the market.

He had prepared his resignation for the county, to be submitted in three months. He figured that was just about enough time for him to put some plans into action that might clean things up a bit and then let him get out of the way before the axe fell on the crooks.

His inspiration about getting information through computers had turned out to be so successful it staggered him. He'd never thought of himself as being all that bright, but Mike Kramer had managed to hack into banking systems and census records, and every possible sort of list all over the world. The boy said he could 'unencrypt' anything anybody could put into cipher codes, whatever that meant.

His quarry had a list of bank accounts, some in the Cayman Islands, and all were coded to numbers that could be traced back, through a web of false identities, to none other than Nathan Farmer, connecting him firmly to Harland Fielding, Oscar Parmelee, and a man named Carlos Monteverde, who now lived in Dallas, Mexico City, and just about any place he chose. Strangely enough, though, he was originally from Templeton, Texas, where his ancestors had settled on a grant from Spain before the Anglos appeared on the horizon. It was the old family account at the smallest bank in Templeton that had given Kramer the clue connecting Monteverde with the other local bad hats.

Ranse didn't understand how Mike managed what he had done, but he now had the printouts locked in the office safe, plus copies mailed to himself in care of his wife's sister. Another set was with an old friend, who swore he'd send them to the Justice Department if anything bad happened to Cole.

The only problem with his scheme was the fact that there was no way to inform Monteverde about what he knew, in order to protect himself. Still, Farmer probably hadn't even told his boss about the local sheriff's rebellion. That would be penny ante stuff to a man like Carlos Monteverde, who was so rich that he considered himself invisible to the law.

Myra opened his office door. 'Chief Shipp is here, Sheriff,' she said. 'Can you see him?'

Cole nodded and straightened his tie. When Shipp entered the office, he looked up, as if he'd been deep in paperwork. 'Wash. Good to see you, man. What can I do for you?'

Shipp looked odd. If Cole didn't know better, he'd think the man was excited, but he'd never seen him flustered by anything before. Now there was a strange gleam in his eye.

Shipp sat in the visitor's chair, his back straight, his regulation hat on his knee, but when he spoke there was an unusual quality in his deep voice. His words were unexpected, too.

'Sheriff, I've known you for years. Never knew you to actually hurt anybody, and I don't think you're crooked, at least not nearly as crooked as some of the people you work for. I'm going to ask you a question, and if your answer satisfies me I'm going to tell you something.'

'And if my answer doesn't satisfy you?' One thing Ranse knew beyond doubt was that Shipp was on the up and up, so this was no act.

'Then I won't tell you what I know. But I think, since your house burned, you've been looking around kind of slow and careful, and I expect you've learned some things. I can maybe add something to that. What do you say?'

Cole thought for a moment. If Shipp was setting him up, there was no hope, anyway. 'Ask away,' he said.

'Do you still have any connection with Harland Fielding or Nate Farmer?'

That was a shock, but he could answer the question truthfully. 'I did do a few favors for Fielding over the years, but never anything really crooked, and nothing that hurt anybody. Recently I cut off the connection all the way, which I figure is the reason my house got bombed. They've got too much nasty stuff they've begun dealin' in to suit me, and I didn't want anything to do with 'em.'

Shipp nodded, his gaze searching Cole's face. He nodded again. 'Can anybody hear us in here?' he whispered.

Cole rose. 'Let's go out and get a cup of coffee, Chief,' he said. Since Kramer showed him how easy it was to listen in on conversations using your own phone system or simply a listening device outside the building, he had become a lot more cautious. 'We'll drive over to Rosie's; let's use your car, if you don't mind. Mine's developed a . . . knock.'

One thing about Washington Shipp, Cole thought. He was quick on the uptake. He rose at once and they went together to the police car parked outside the courthouse. Only when they were beyond the main part of town, turning down the quiet street on which Rosie's café was situated, did he sigh and speak.

'Now we can talk, Wash. What's goin' on?'

Shipp chose his words carefully. 'Sheriff, I was down in the river bottoms Sunday. Took a boy I know there fishin'. We got turned around — you know better than anybody how you can do that, under those thick treetops — and then we heard a helicopter, moving back and forth across the bottomlands.'

He seemed to expect some reply, so Cole nodded. 'Been there many a time and got lost more than I stayed found. So what was that chopper lookin' for, do you know?'

'Well, it seemed like it might be scanning for plantings of marijuana, but when it came by real low and close to a little clearing, I could see Nate Farmer in the passenger's side.'

He cocked his head, and now Cole knew something big was on its way.

'Farmer, eh? If he was down there, it's ninety to nothing he was lookin' for that stash those dead men lost there this summer. Which tells me he was the one they was supposed to deliver it to. So what then?' For it was clear the story was not finished.

'I wondered, after I got a glimpse of Farmer, just what was going on, so I got the boy to go with me and we followed it, till it started to hover over a sinkhole. You know how many of those there are in the swamp, and this was a big one. Biggest I ever saw or heard of. We crept up to a thick spot that would hide us and watched while the chopper started sort of trolling with a black box kind of device, going lower and lower. And then, out of the blue, I heard a terrible crack, and one blade of the chopper bent, and the whole thing went down and sank out of sight quicker than it takes to tell the tale. I've been figuring about it ever since, and it seems to me it must be a blade hit a tree branch and broke.'

Cole stared at Shipp, who by then was turning into the parking lot of the café. There was more to it than that, he would have bet his best socks, but he'd never get it out of the chief.

'You mean Nate Farmer's gone? Just like that?' he said. 'Why, that would mean the county fathers would have to find an entirely new Big Crook to manage all the little crooks they control.'

Inside he was thinking it also meant that Carlos Monteverde, on losing his inside man, might find it necessary to visit Templeton. Which could make things interesting.

Shipp parked neatly and killed the engine. 'Yessir, Farmer's gone, with whoever was piloting that chopper. We were lost, you remember, and it took us the rest of the day to find our way out. By then, neither the boy nor I could have found that spot again in a million years. And of course, the men in the craft were long dead. Then it occurred to me that this might not be such a bad thing.

'With Farmer gone, just like that, a lot of loose ends in his business are going to start to unravel, particularly since none of his people are going to have a clue what happened to him. Fielding isn't an idea man, just a strong-arm, and I figure a smart lawman might get some information out of him if he went at it right. Farmer wasn't the biggest Big Man, either, but likely he did all the thinking for his bunch. But of course, *you* know more about him than I do, being as he's out of my jurisdiction.'

Cole began to grin. 'Wash, let's just keep this between us for the time being. Let Farmer's henchmen get nervous when he don't turn up. Folks make mistakes when they're off-balance, and when nobody knows what happened they're going to be off-balance, big time.'

He opened his door and joined Shipp as he went into the café. Over coffee they just made small talk. The biggest gossips in Templeton drank coffee at Rosie's most of the day and part of the night. Retired men didn't have much to occupy their minds, and anything said at Rosie's, even in a whisper, was public knowledge two hours later.

When Shipp dropped him back at his office, Cole called Myra in and closed the door. 'Get me Deputy Philips,' he wrote on her steno pad. 'And don't say anything aloud unless you want it known all over. I think we may be bugged.'

She looked shocked and he knew she suddenly had realized how some things they both thought were secrets had found their way outside the office.

'Got some filin' for you to do, Myra,' he said aloud. 'I think I'll go home and see how the workmen are doing. If anything comes up, you can call me on that cell phone.'

'Yes, sir,' she said, but she wrote, 'Shall I send Philips over there?'

He nodded and left the office, hearing file drawers open and close. She'd do that for a bit and then find some reason to leave so she could alert Philips.

At home, he found one carpenter ripping out burned carpet to get to the floorboards of the living room. Another was on the roof, removing melted asphalt shingles.

'You want to replace this with something fire-proof?' the man called down. 'It's a wonder the whole roof didn't go up.'

Cole thought for a moment. 'You know, let's put on a new roof. It'll have to be done in a year or two, anyway. You know that colored metal roofing? That'd be good. Fireproof. What's the price?'

'Higher than this cheap stuff.'

'Go the whole hog,' Cole said. 'Insurance will pay for most of it, anyway, and if I have the place in good shape it'll be easier to sell.'

He made his way around the yard, watering the grass and checking Mae's flowers, though she wouldn't see them bloom here next year, if he had any luck selling out.

He was staring at the workshop he'd built years before but had never had the time to use when Philips pulled up in the driveway. 'You need me, Sheriff Cole?' he asked.

Cole looked around. In the daytime, there was nobody at home in this neighborhood except those too old to work, but this was his own house, and it, too, might be bugged in some way.

'Let's go for a walk, Deputy,' he said, heading toward the sidewalk. 'I've got somethin' I need for you to do . . .'

13

Fishing in Deep Water

Washington thought hard about his interview with the sheriff as he drove back to his office. As soon as he finished with the stack of paperwork waiting for him, he leaned back in his chair, which had been comfortably broken in by his predecessor over decades of service, and thought long and hard.

He knew he hadn't been entirely straightforward with Cole. Over his own years of sitting in this chair, he had run across a lot of sticky trails that led to Nate Farmer and, beyond him, to a shadowy figure who looked more and more like Carlos, the last of the fabled Monteverdes. There were other bad hats in town, of course, but they were small potatoes compared with Carlos. Wash had compiled a considerable dossier on the man, using federal facilities when he could and even Interpol, once, when he had done a favor for the police in Dallas and they offered him the chance. He was certain there were Colombian connections, and there had been a mention from Interpol of a Libyan connection as well. That might explain the possibility of something valuable, and even dangerous, in that shipment.

He scooted his chair on its rollers and fetched up against the filing cabinet at the back corner of his tiny office. Here he kept things unconnected with ongoing cases, yet which he felt would be convenient to have at hand. He took out that file and stared at it, turning the pages of printout. Then he took the bundle into the file room and photocopied the entire thing. Ransom Cole might be able to use this, and together they might stand a chance of nailing someone bigger than a tadpole like Harland Fielding.

Cole's caution as they talked together had impressed him, so he told nobody that he was copying the file. He'd wrap it in with the bunch of reports that was ready to go, and he'd deliver it himself to

Cole's girl, Myra, when he drove home.

Before he sealed the parcel, he wrote a note on a file card and inserted it into the dossier. That should set the sheriff's gears in motion, he thought.

The next morning, he had been inspecting a robbery scene when his radio in the official car sputtered and his dispatcher said, 'Chief Shipp, could you swing by the courthouse on your way back to the office? Somebody there wants to check some things out with you.'

Wash gave a deep sigh. Matters were about to move, he felt sure. He wasn't at all surprised when Myra waved him down as he drove up outside the courthouse.

'Sheriff Cole asked if you'd drive over to the high school and meet him there,' she said. 'He has a problem that's come up and thinks you might be able to handle it.' She took the file he handed to her through the window and waved him on his way.

He passed the sheriff's marked car, which was parked beside the street two blocks from the high school. Pulling up ahead of it, he gestured for Cole to join him, which he did without wasting time.

'Run up toward the river,' Cole said. 'I need to get our ducks in a row here.'

Wash turned toward the park that flanked the river some blocks ahead, and when he came to the first entrance he turned in and stopped, facing the coffee-colored water. The place was deserted at this time of day, and the two of them got out of the car and went down the path along the edge of the stream. The mutter of water amid and over rocks and around thick growths of cattails would cover their conversation.

'I've got several things on my plate,' Cole said. 'First off, I've had a boy checking into computer files all over the place, and we've got some pretty solid stuff on Carlos Monteverde.'

Wash grunted. 'I kind of thought he might be mixed up in our last mess, back in the summer. What else?'

'I been thinking about the way that fellow Parker came in here like he was God a 'mighty and pushed folks around. While I had this boy workin', I got him to look into Parker's business as well.' He looked sideways at Wash and winked. 'Tax business, you know.'

Shipp almost swallowed his tongue. Now why did someone like Ranse Cole ever think of hacking into bank and government records? His estimation of the man's intelligence went up several notches, though he knew what had been done was completely illegal. Still, when you dealt with crooks, sometimes you had to get your hands dirty.

Cole grinned like a possum and went on, 'We found some interestin' stuff. I think a good case could be made for auditing his income taxes — say back to 1987. That's when things started to look suspicious. So I've sent a letter to the IRS people. I think Parker will be too busy pulling his own feet out of the fire to worry about anything back here.'

Wash sighed deeply. Even if the means weren't quite kosher, the end was one he could agree with. 'Okay. Anything else?'

Cole looked uncomfortable. 'You know, Wash, I been around here all my life. Never took much stock in the fairytales folks tell about . . . certain people in the swamp. But you never know, do you? Might be somethin' in the tales. I been wondering if that old lady down there, Miz Lena, could help us, maybe.'

Shipp looked him in the eye. 'Ranse, that old lady can do just about anything she decides to. Tell me what you need for her to do, and I'll see about getting word to her. I have lots of kinfolk down in the low country.'

Cole began to outline what he needed. As he finished speaking, Shipp grinned, reached for his hand and shook it heartily. 'I never thought of you as being in that class, Ranse, but you surprise me. For *sneaky*, this beats all. And it isn't really mean, either, because the folks that will suffer deserve to but never will, left to the law. I'll get the word out as soon as I can.'

★ ★ ★

Wim Dooley had not forgotten the thing he had witnessed beside the sinkhole. Seeing someone die in that particular way made him unusually quiet and thoughtful all week, making his mother believe he was taking sick. She had no experience of sick children — of all her brood, none had ever so much as had the sniffles, and he could tell she was worried. He couldn't tell her about it, though. He'd promised Chief Shipp that he'd talk only to lawmen, if they ever came down and asked, and even then he'd stick to the story they'd put together as they trudged back to the car.

Finally his ma consulted Miz Libby, who had dosed generations of children in the brakes with sassafras and willow-bark teas, plantain poultices, and all sorts of herbal remedies the medicos had never dreamed might be useful.

The old woman looked Wim over and shook her head. 'Miz Dooley, somethin's worryin' that child. Just let him loose a bit to work it out. He's a sensible boy, and he'll come out of it on his own. No use gummin' up his innards with medicine when all he needs is some time.'

That relieved Wim a bit, though his ma seemed to think that if you didn't take medicine you couldn't cure the problem. However, she took Miz Libby's advice to heart and let him stay home from school on Friday. She even let him walk up to the store to spend some of her precious quarters on a cold bottle of pop.

As he crossed Miz Libby's front yard, he glimpsed a familiar vehicle sitting under the sycamore tree on the far side of the house. Now what was Chief Shipp doing out here this time of the week? Wim struggled with himself — only for a second or two, but he did struggle — before running around to the back door and knocking softly.

Shipp himself came to the door and stood staring down at Wim as if he might be a ghost. 'Boy, how'd you know I wanted to get a message to you?' he asked, opening the rusted screen to let him in.

Wim shook his head. 'I didn't know, but Ma let me stay home today and she even give me this.' He held out a grimy palm with two quarters staring up like silvery eyes. 'And here you was, so I came to find out if anythin' has happened.'

'Not yet.' Shipp opened Miz Libby's refrigerator and took out a bottle of orange juice, from which he poured a generous glassful. 'But with your help, it's going to start. I need to know a couple of things, and it's mighty important. I know you keep secrets — I did the same when I was your age — but this is no game. It's for real. So will you answer me, straight up and no lies, if I ask you some questions?'

Feeling somewhat overwhelmed, Wim nodded and sat in the chair Miz Libby had set for him by her table. He swallowed hard and waited for the questions, his knees feeling a bit quivery.

'You know Possum Choa . . . do you know where he lives?'

Wim gulped again. That was the main secret of his life, and he had always felt a sacred obligation not to tell anyone that information.

'I don't want to know *where*,' Shipp reassured him. 'If you do know, just nod.'

That was better, so Wim nodded, a short jerk of his chin.

'Can Choa read?' was the next question.

Again Wim nodded. 'He even knows

275

about the old Romans and how they took over back in England, long years ago.'

Shipp looked surprised, but he looked pleased, too. 'Then you won't have to memorize the message I need to get to him. My last question is this: Can you take this to him as quick as possible this afternoon? Will your ma let you go?'

Wim considered. 'I can get there, no problem, but gettin' Ma to let me into the swamp again may be hard. If you was to go with me and ask, she would, for certain.'

Which was why, before mid-afternoon, Wim was halfway across the stretch of swamp lying between the brakes and Choa's cabin. When Chief Shipp set himself to persuade an anxious mother, he was very good at it. Wim decided he would have to practice that himself. It might come in handy, in time to come.

Long before he came in sight of the isolated hut, he gave a shrill whistle that set every crow in sight cawing warnings. Choa would know somebody was coming, and Wim was pretty sure he'd know who.

He wasn't disappointed. In another half hour he saw a dark shape moving silkily along the shadowy ridge he was following, ducking beneath trailing hanks of Spanish moss and sidling along narrow spots.

'Possum Choa?' he called, just to let the man know he was there and was a friend.

'Young Wim? What you doin' here, boy? Anything wrong down your way?'

'Nossir.'

Wim stopped to wait for him to come up. Then he said, 'I got a letter for you from Chief Shipp, from over to Templeton. He says it's mighty important, so we better find a good place to stop so you can read it.'

Choa cocked his grizzled head, as if listening to a far-off voice. Then he said, 'You come back to the house with me, Wim. I got stew and cornbread all cooked up and ready for supper. Does your ma know where you be? If she don't, I'll take you home myself when our business is done.'

Wim felt a huge joy fill him from toes

to scalp. 'She knows. Chief Shipp told her I'd prob'ly have to spend the night, so she won't worry. Let's go.'

To spend the night with Possum Choa, on a mission so important even his ma understood . . . Never had he thought anything so wonderful could happen to him.

He followed Choa into the dimness, and before the sun sank they sat together over a burning pine-knot, reading the letter Shipp had written hastily on a school tablet Miz Libby used for making grocery lists.

Things were about to happen, and Wim had not suspected how grave they were when he undertook his mission.

As he dropped off to sleep on Choa's spare quilt on the floor, he knew this was something he would never forget, no matter if he lived to be forty years old!

★   ★   ★

His business had gone so well for so long that it disturbed Carlos Monteverde to find such a serious lapse in his command structure. He had thought it foolproof, though he had envied the fear factor his Colombian connections could command.

Nate Farmer's unexplained absence, along with the disappearance of the helicopter belonging to his son, was bad enough. But the complete loss of the shipment, vital to the new, more dangerous interests he found himself representing, was much worse. That was what brought him back to home territory in a hurry.

He flew into Dallas in a corporate jet belonging to a business not obviously associated with his own interests, landing at Love Field rather than DFW. There the car he had ordered met him, but he dismissed the driver. When the time came to attend to business of this magnitude, the fewer people involved the better.

This would not be the first time he had killed, if it came to that, and on his own ground there was no one better at hiding the traces than Carlos Monteverde.

He headed east and south, using the old federal highways. Along these back roads there were few highway patrolmen and little traffic, which suited him well. Though the car was licensed to another business entirely, and his own appearance was not his usual one, Carlos left no detail to chance. He kept his speed just beneath the posted limit, and he slowed as he passed through the few tiny towns on his route. He wanted no outside interference.

Harland Fielding was going to have to die, just as soon as he could manage it, and he wanted no suspicion that he was in the area at all. With Farmer gone, Fielding was too weak a reed to risk, and it was certain the local lawmen would lean on him soon. A trade like Monteverde's left few clues, but inevitably there would be some, and low-level flunkies like Fielding always knew more than they were supposed to.

He slid through Templeton at dusk and turned onto the old highway leading to the homestead where his ancestors once had lived. The house now looked desolate, and no light showed through its dusty windows, yet he knew the rooms were kept clean and prepared for his arrival at any time.

He smiled into the darkness, feeling the cut-over woods give way to the thick growth as he neared the river. By instinct as much as by sight, he turned off the gravel road into the double track that marked the approach to the house. The old cypress building was hidden by thick stands of timber and heavy growths of brush and berry vines.

The track turned sharply, and in the concealed garden he saw that the grass had been cut, bushes trimmed back, and the graveled path swept. Old Conchita lived in a shanty on the road, and every day she came to keep the home place in shape. A check came to her each month from a company no one could trace if they tried. When she died, he was either going to have to abandon this ancestral hideaway or find someone equally needy and fearful to take over her duties.

The air was chilly, for it was early winter now, and the atmosphere was heavy with damp. He killed the engine, after pulling the car into a slump-roofed shed, and reached back for his suitcase.

He knew the house would be warm, for he paid to have wood hauled each year to Conchita's house, and she brought carloads to the old house regularly during the winter, in order to keep the wood furnace simmering to keep out the damp.

The door opened easily when he turned his key in the lock. The air was cool but not cold, and he set his case down and went into the back to open the dampers and add more wood to the furnace. Food waited in the humming refrigerator, all fresh, for Conchita used up anything that waited very long and replaced it with new supplies. He boiled eggs, toasted bread, microwaved bacon. The house might look a wreck from outside, but inside it had everything he needed.

After a long trip, made harder by worry, he knew he must eat and rest. Tomorrow he would get in touch with his information sources and learn just what had gone so wrong, where he had always felt himself to be invulnerable. He had ties here that went back for generations, and those who were not devoted to him personally were terrified of him. It was an excellent context for his business deals.

As he stretched between crisp sheets in the great bed where his great-great-grandfather once had slept, he found himself relaxing at last.

Just as he felt himself drifting into sleep, a thought nudged him awake again. Why had he felt compelled to come back and attend to this personally? He had people he could send to do the work. They were competent, good at covering their tracks. Yet a few days after he heard of Farmer's disappearance, he had felt literally pushed into action. By the end of a week he could no longer resist the urge to come home again . . . almost as if someone had willed him to return.

Nonsense! Carlos turned on his side and yawned. No one could compel Carlos Monteverde to do anything. His father could not. His mother had tried, God knew, and failed. His grandfather had used a gold-headed walking stick on him as a child, without changing any element of his spirit. He had been self-willed since he came from the womb, and no one would ever make him do anything he did not choose to do. Even the priest, urged by the womenfolk to save this errant boy, had admitted defeat at last. The memory was pure pleasure to Carlos.

Thinking that, smiling faintly, he fell asleep at last.

* * *

The forest was thick, and there were no traces of the work of loggers. The trees were fat and their branches made a high roof against the invisible stars. Still, his feet knew, without faltering, the faint trail they followed, and he did not seem to need to see.

After a time, he began to recognize the winding of the stream he followed, the jut of a great red rock from the deep leaf-mold, the curve of a tree that had endured even since his childhood. He was walking into the swamp country, finding the all but invisible ridges as he went.

It had been cold before, but now he felt the steamy warmth of decomposition rising around him. The yeasty smell of the great sinkhole met his nostrils. He must be very near the spot where for centuries it had sucked down everything touching its surface.

Carlos stopped and shook his head roughly, trying to wake, trying to pull himself back into his sleeping body, for he knew now that he dreamed. He could not awaken. Something — some will far older and stronger than his own — forced him to go on, to step carefully through the mosquito- and gnat-infested bushes, past the pools where water moccasins slithered through the mud.

As he drew near the morass, he felt something inside him curdle with fear. He had never come here by night, even as a daring boy, and now he found that the thought of being drawn there against his will filled him with a cold dread. Still his dream-self moved forward, unable to turn aside or to go back. The Spanish moss dangling from low branches brushed across his face, and he stooped to pass beneath. Then he stood on the edge of the still pool that topped the quagmire, seeing the moon reflected from its murky mirror.

His black nana, when he was small, used to tell him tales of that sinkhole, describing the way it sucked down any unwary creature. She had told him that it turned, once in a long while, sending long-digested contents into the light again. Skulls of deer, bones of anonymous animals, turtle shells — her description of the strange things that rose, only to sink again into the muck, had made his young blood run cold.

He stood at the edge of the quagmire, watching it turn. He had heard a hiss and looked down to see a snake coiled at his feet. He had shrieked voicelessly as the moccasin struck, only to fall through his intangible leg and sprawl on the dark soil . . .

The sound of sucking waters, hissing bubbles, and roiling mud now made him look out over the expanse. The sinkhole was turning. He found he could not close his eyes or bend his neck to stare at the ground. As he watched, glistening lumps bubbled to the surface, some horned, some grinning vacantly.

He gasped for breath, clenched his

hands, willed himself to wake or at least to look away, but he could not. A log came to the surface, its butt at least ten feet in diameter. It had been generations since such a log was cut down here. This great tree must have fallen before his ancestors came to the swamp country.

A thin vane thrust itself into the air, dripping slime. The thing was connected to a rod, other vanes, the shape of a helicopter, and all rose together, turning as the swamp turned, only to sink again. A face stared out of the muck for a moment, and despite the work of mortal decay, it was recognizable. Nate Farmer, missing no longer, paid a last visit to the open air and sank again. His narrow jaw, crooked teeth, and long forehead had been unmistakable

Carlos tried to scream, tried to groan, but he could do neither.

Now he shrieked at last, this time with a voice rising from his own throat, and he woke to find himself tangled in the sheets, dripping with sweat. He staggered into the bathroom, washed his face, drank bottled water, and took one of his rare sleeping doses. Usually he slept like the dead . . . He shook away the thought.

He turned on the bedside lamp and looked at the clock. Two in the morning. What had caused that dream? Had Nate actually gone down into the sinkhole? And why should he have gone there in the first place?

Unless . . . unless he had learned, somehow, that the chest was there, along with its vital contents. Carlos went into the kitchen and got his notebook from his briefcase.

Check on Farmer's brother. Has chopper. What were they doing?

Then he returned to bed. Tomorrow he would learn just what Farmer had been doing there, and that would show him where the merchandise must be.

★ ★ ★

This time he sank even more deeply into the dream. He was struggling with a tangle of vines that had trapped his feet. As he thrashed, grasping at overhead branches, he found himself at the verge of the quagmire, and before he could accept that as fact, he had toppled into the black mire.

Headfirst he sank, turned desperately upright, and tried to remember how to survive quicksand. Lie flat — that was it. He stretched his arms wide, raised his feet, and found himself floating on top of the muck.

He grinned at the patch of stars between the overhanging boughs. The grin froze on his face as he felt something squirm against his side, slither past his head, touch the side of his face. The place was alive with snakes! If he moved, the moccasins would bite him, and he would die. If he didn't move, he would sink into the hole, down there with Nate Farmer and that slimy helicopter — and die.

A coil wrapped about his ankle and tugged it downward. Another looped about his neck, forcing his head beneath the slick of water. He held his breath as he sank, pulled down by invisible snakes, and as he went he seemed to see faint glimmers of phosphorescence surrounding terrible shapes.

Snakes were his tremendous phobia. But Carlos was also claustrophobic. The combination of terrors was beyond endurance, and he lost himself in a maelstrom of blackness and fear.

14

A Job Well Done

Lena McCarver woke with a grunt. At her feet, Lone raised his head, stretched, and yawned. She sat, easing her aching bones as she moved, and nodded to the cat. 'Good job, Cat,' she said. 'Sending a vision is a lot easier said than done, I can tell you.' She groaned upright and washed her face in her cracked china bowl. Spluttering, she dried herself, dressed, and went into the kitchen to make strong coffee.

'Takes it out of me,' she said. 'Cat, I'm just not the woman I was, and that's the plain truth. Now I've got to raise the signal on the tree so King can come get the word. Can't leave that young idiot to die there in his own bed. Drat!'

She limped to the porch, moved around the house and out her back gate, and climbed the knoll to the great pine tree. The yellow signal flag tried to hang up a couple of times on its way up, but a good yank from Lena loosed it and shot it to the top. Then she made her way back to the kitchen, where she fixed a huge breakfast to recharge her drained energies. She fed Lone two cans of tuna fish, for he was no spring chicken, either.

Once both had eaten, they sat on the porch, Lone melting into the top step, Lena lying back in the swing, which moved just enough to soothe her mind and settle her temper. They dozed half the morning, until a distant hail woke them.

Possum Choa was coming down the hill behind the house, walking faster than usual. 'You done it?' he said. 'You actually done it.'

Behind him Lena could see Wim, half running to keep up with Choa's longer legs. 'Glad you brought the boy,' she said. 'Sit and eat a cookie before you start back. You, boy, you want some water to cool you off?'

Wim nodded, eyes wide, but he was too

intimidated at being in the presence of the old lady to say a word. Lena handed him a bunch of cookies and turned to Choa. 'He's at his house, probably out of it for good. He had a bad dream, I think, and his conscience did the rest. Carlos Monteverde isn't likely to do any more mischief for a long time, if ever. You get the word to somebody who can go get him and take him to town and get him treated.'

Wim came to life. 'Chief Shipp! I kin cut through the woods west of the swamp and get to Miz Libby's. She'll go to the store and call him. She kin have him out there before the sun goes down.'

She grinned at him. 'Good work, boy.' Then she squinted her eyes. 'You ever have any time to work outside the family? I'm getting old, and sometimes I have things I can't do anymore. You come over in the summertime, and I can keep you busy. Pay you a bit, too.'

Wim began to smile. 'You mean it? The other kids are big enough to help Ma, if I could make a little bit of cash money. I think I could get her to say yes. You've got a good name with the folks in the brakes. Miz Libby says you taught her all she knows about medicine plants.'

Choa rose, dusting cookie crumbs from his lap. 'We got to go, young Wim. We'll get word to Chief Shipp, Miz Lena. You can rest easy about that.'

They trudged off together, and Lena laughed to see how closely the boy tried to imitate Choa's loose gait. That young Wim was a boy to watch . . . one to teach. If he'd work for her a bit, she could give him some guidance that might come in handy along the way.

She sighed. Old Possum wouldn't last forever, nor would King — nor would she. It would be a pure pity to leave the swamp country without someone who knew the old ways and could keep an eye on what went on down here.

With all the devilment goin' on in the outside world, some was bound to spill over into the bottomlands. Needed to be somebody to put spokes in their wheels, once the old crew was gone.

★ ★ ★

Wash got the call just before he left his office. Aunt Libby sounded excited, and he pricked up his ears.

'Got word from somebody you know, Wash. Says you need to go out to the old Monteverde place, out past Polywash Creek, and check on Carlos Monteverde. He has a . . . problem . . . and may need to go to the hospital. You got that clear?' she asked.

Shipp felt the glow of satisfaction. 'She did it, Aunt Libby. The old lady did it! I never quite thought it would work, but by golly she managed it somehow.'

'Don't tell me what she did, Nephew, 'cause I don't want to know. But if you mean Miz Lena, she kin do just about anything she sets her mind to, and don't you never forget that. Now scat!'

Shipp hung up and sat back in his deep chair. He stared at the phone for a moment. Then he picked it up again and punched in the sheriff's office number.

'Myra? Is Cole there?'

There was a click, and Ranse's voice asked, 'What kin I do for you, Chief?'

'You want to take a little jaunt out in

the country with me? That project you asked me about the other day — I think it may have come off. You want to find out?'

There was a grunt at the other end of the line. Then the sheriff said, his tone carefully unexcited, 'Might as well. Want to go in my car? I still got a ping in the county one.'

'Pick me up in fifteen minutes,' Shipp told him and stood to put on his jacket. The day was turning cool, and even in the low country it would be uncomfortable.

The leaves were brown now, and the grass had been tanned by the first big frost last week. Cole drove fast, sometimes using his detachable flasher to get around slow traffic. When they turned off on the farm road, then onto the county road, he slowed, and Wash began to look for the obscure track leading to the old Monteverde place.

Fresh tire tracks marked the damp soil. He looked at Cole, who nodded and turned in, following the drive around the thick growth and onto the gravel patch amid the mown grass. The track they followed led straight to a shed, whose dark interior showed the shape of a car.

'He's here, all right,' Cole said, drawing his pistol.

'He's here, but he's not here,' Wash replied. 'If Aunt Libby is right, which she always is, he has *problems*. That means he isn't going to know or care much about what we do. I gave pretty specific suggestions, when I sent word to Miz McCarver, and I understand she's mighty good at doing what's needed.'

He stepped onto the back stoop to find the door unlocked. Even after so many years of living in cities, Carlos evidently still had the country instinct to leave his house open. Out here in the boonies, nobody would dream of bothering a neighbor, and this house was so hidden that fishermen going to the river or the creek would never know it was here.

Shipp opened the door and went in, to find the house warm, with the smell of food still hanging in the kitchen. He moved up the hall to find the bedroom door open, as well. There he stopped and gestured for Cole to come up beside him.

'Look!' he murmured.

They stood together, watching the man on the bed, who was flailing his arms desperately, as if drowning. When Cole stepped up to touch his shoulder, the dark eyes opened and stared up at him.

'The snakes! Get them away from me! And the quicksand — oh, it's covering my face! Help! Help me!'

Those eyes plainly did not see them — or the room. Carlos Monteverde was lost in some terrible context that was now his own reality.

Together, the two men got him into his clothing and half carried him, still struggling against his private nightmares, to the car.

'You think he'll come out of this?' Cole asked.

'If my auntie is right, he won't — or if he does, he'll be too old to make any waves,' the chief replied.

'Good,' Cole grunted and started the car.

★   ★   ★

The crickets had gone silent with the passing of autumn. Many birds had migrated south, though the cardinals and jays still showed glints of crimson and blue amid the leafless branches of the forest as they searched for food. Crows filled the chill air with their raucous calls, and buzzards circled overhead on their constant search for the dead and dying.

Possum Choa liked every season there was, cold or hot, wet or dry. He particularly liked it when the bottomlands settled into their winter state, quieter than the rest of the year and yet with enough activity to keep him interested.

Like the squirrels, now buried in their untidy nests and tree-hollows, he had stored up food for the cold months, though he could always wade out and dredge up cattail roots or mussels if he wanted to. His ground corn, dried fruit and tomatoes, and the wheat flour he traded for with some of the farmers along the river, would last him until spring.

When he wanted meat, he could go possum or coon hunting, or he might find a bunch of piney-woods rooters and add pork to his menu. But he needn't do that if he didn't want to. Flapjacks, honey from the bee tree he had robbed last summer, and nuts gathered beneath the hickories and chinquapin trees would keep an old man fed and healthy for a long time.

He was sitting on his porch, staring out over the muted shades of the winter swamp. The water was pewter-gray, reflecting the incoming clouds that promised rain soon. The wood beyond combined shades of gray as well, lit by an occasional bright leaf left over from fall.

He was thinking about the bump and the cry he had heard, back last summer, and all the strange happenings that had followed since then. It was a weird world, after all, and because he had been listening, a bad thing had been stopped in its tracks.

A soft step brought him to his feet, and he peered along the track beside the water. A small shape waved, and Choa began to chuckle. 'So you found me, young Wim. Thought you might,' he said.

'Oh, I found you a long time ago, Possum Choa,' the boy said. 'Just didn't think you could feel you could trust me much, then. Now I think maybe it won't bother you. Anyway, I got some news for you.'

Choa gestured for Wim to sit beside him. He pitched a chip toward the dock, and it clattered on the ancient wood. 'Got word about that message we took to Miz Lena? I been wonderin' about that, how it come out.' He looked down at the tow-head lad close to his shoulder. If his own boy had lived . . . But he pushed that thought out of his mind.

Wim pitched a chip of his own, imitating Choa's movements faithfully. 'Yep, Chief Shipp come out yesterday to tell us. Said Miz Lena fetched some dreams for that man that sent him right over the edge. He's in the crazy-house at Rusk now. Can't do a thing for hisself. Chief Shipp waited till the doctors had a look at him and had their say before he brought us word. They think he'll be there, wrastlin' snakes and tryin' not to drown, as long as he lives. That's a right nasty thought, ain't it?'

Choa stared at the gray water amid the cattail stalks, thinking how it would be to spend eternity trying to push away water moccasins. 'Druther be dead,' he said.

'Me too,' said Wim Dooley.

They sat in silence while night came down over the swamp country, and darkness blotted out the dimples as rain began to fall on the water.

'Spend the night?' Choa asked. 'I kind of thought you might like to do some tale-tellin' with me this winter. You seem likely to be a swamp runner like me, and there's things I can teach you.'

Wim nodded. 'Ma said it was all right. And Chief Shipp said tell you he's mighty glad you did what you did.' He rose to follow Choa into the rickety cabin. 'Me, too,' he added. 'I hope, time I'm your age, there won't be such mean critters comin' into the swamp. I'd rather have snakes and gators, any day of the week.'

Possum closed the door and poked up the smolder of fire on the hearth. They dropped to sit before the blaze, and Choa thought back to his own father and grandfather.

'We got a lot of ground to cover,' he began. 'So let's get started . . . '

We do hope that you have enjoyed reading this large print book.

Did you know that all of our titles are available for purchase?

We publish a wide range of high quality large print books including:
Romances, Mysteries, Classics
General Fiction
Non Fiction and Westerns

Special interest titles available in large print are:
The Little Oxford Dictionary
Music Book, Song Book
Hymn Book, Service Book

Also available from us courtesy of Oxford University Press:
Young Readers' Dictionary
(large print edition)
Young Readers' Thesaurus
(large print edition)

For further information or a free brochure, please contact us at:
Ulverscroft Large Print Books Ltd.,
The Green, Bradgate Road, Anstey,
Leicester, LE7 7FU, England.
Tel: (00 44) 0116 236 4325
Fax: (00 44) 0116 234 0205

THE GALLOWS IN MY GARDEN

Richard Deming

Grace Lawson and her brother Donald stand to inherit their late father's millions when they reach the age of twenty-one — but someone in their household of family, servants and regular guests seems intent on ensuring they don't live that long. Donald disappears, and a would-be killer dogs Grace's every move. Not wanting to involve the police and create a family scandal, Grace turns to private investigator Manville Moon — who is unaware of how complex the case will be, or that his own life will be threatened . . .

IT'S HER FAULT

Tony Gleeson

An aging university professor insists to Detective Frank Vandegraf that his estranged wife is trying to kill him, but the problem is that she's nowhere to be found. A relative claims that it's the other way around: the husband is actually threatening to kill his wife. When the professor turns up murdered shortly thereafter, with a mysterious note lying on his chest that says 'IT'S HER FAULT', Frank redoubles his efforts to locate the missing wife, his prime suspect. But when he does, the case becomes even more baffling . . .